THE LEAD SOLDIERS

URI ORLEV

The Lead Soldiers

A NOVEL

Translated from the Hebrew

by Hillel Halkin

TAPLINGER PUBLISHING COMPANY
New York

First published in the United States in 1980 by
TAPLINGER PUBLISHING CO., INC.
New York, New York

Copyright © 1956 by Uri Orlev

English translation © 1979/The Institute for the Translation of
Hebrew Literature Ltd.

Library of Congress Cataloging in Publication Data
Orlev, Uri
  The lead soldiers.

  Translation of Hayale-oferet.
  I. Title.
PZ4.O7146Le   1980   [PJ5054.O74]   892.4'3'6   79-26348
ISBN 0-8008-4576-5

THE LEAD SOLDIERS

PROLOGUE

The hero of this story, which is more than half true, is a small boy who hadn't seen very much of anything in his life, which may be why he wasn't afraid to see more. The war swept him from one place to another, yet he still always found room to put down his toy soldiers. No one could keep him from striding about the globe with seven-league boots.

The boy was the son of a young couple who lived in Warsaw. His father, Doctor M. M. Kosowolski, was a graduate of the medical school there, a radiologist. His mother Sofia, now Pani Kosowolska, received her degree in chemistry from the same university in Warsaw, but after her marriage devoted herself to family life. Though both she and her husband came from well-to-do, observant Jewish homes, both were attracted in their teens to the fashionable leftism of the times, and did their best to forget and even conceal their Jewish origins.

Their first son was named Jerzy Henryk. Jerzy Henryk Kosowolski. Eight days after his birth his grandfather had him circumcised despite the strenuous protests of his parents. Their second son was listed on his birth certificate as Kazimierz Stefan, apparently in honour of King Kazimierz the Great. This time, too, the boy's grandparents were forced to act as surrogates for his ancestral religion.

Jerzy Henryk began life with a near fatal case of

meningitis, which he survived despite the thousand-to-one odds against it at the time. Equally stunned by his illness and his miraculous recovery, his parents moved to the village of Radosczi outside Warsaw and proceeded to bring him up overprotectively. The two boys lived in a world that consisted, apart from their parents, of a rarely-changing governess, a frequently-changing cleaning woman, and for a brief while, a lady French tutor, who was skinny like all lady French tutors. Next came their uncles, aunts and cousins, whose importance was measured by the presents they gave and the stories they could tell.

'Kazik the red!' Jerzy would tease his ginger-haired brother.

'You're as black as a Jew, Yurik!' Kazimierz would retort.

Neither of them knew yet that he was a Jew. How could they have? No one had bothered to inform them. When all Poland celebrated Christmas, they too had a large, splendidly decorated fir tree in their house, beneath which were hidden the gifts that white-bearded Saint Nikolai had brought them. Ask either boy which was his right hand, and he would cross himself and say: 'This one.'

Jerzy Henryk Kosowolski began his formal education at the local nursery school, where he stood like the other children with his apron on and prayed trustingly with palms together to the good crucified Jesus, the Holy Mother of God, and the guardian angel who watched over children.

> Watchful angel, angel mine,
> Who guards me where my steps incline,
> Morning, evening, afternoon.

In the name of the Father, the Son and the Holy Ghost, the nursery school teacher guided his little hand over his

6

heart and forehead and taught him the sign of the cross.

When Yurik was a little older, his family moved to Zoliboz, a new suburb of Warsaw, so that he might attend the school there. Here our story begins.

I

Sofia awoke and glanced at the clock. It was still early. She got out of bed and hurried to the window.

The light of the street lamps faded into the light of the dawn. Clusters of people, heavily burdened, were moving quickly in the direction of the city.

She opened the window and leaned out. For a long while she looked at the people in the street before calling anxiously:

'Excuse me there! Where are you going?'

Someone looked up and replied:

'To the city, Pani Doctor. They say that it's safer there.'

Sofia shut the window and hurried to the children's room.

'Yurik, Kazhiula, it's time to get up. We can't stay here any longer.'

The elder brother opened his eyes first. 'Are we going away?' he asked sleepily.

'If we can find something to go in. Get a move on! We have to try to get to Father's clinic.'

Yurik sat up in bed and listened.

'Mama, there are a lot of people outside.'

'That's right,' she said.

'Is Papa coming too?'

'Your father is in the army. Have you forgotten, young man?'

'Can I take his officer's cap?'

'I'll put it in a special place for you here,' she promised. 'You'll get it when we come back. Sit on the toilet.'

'I've already gone.'

9

'Are you sure? I don't want any trouble on the way.'
She lowered the boy to the floor.

'Mama!' he complained, searching for his shoes.

'Look under the bed,' she told him.

She dressed her younger son and went to pack.

'Yurik! Come here for a minute and sit on top of the suitcase. You too,' she called to his brother. 'As hard as you can.'

The suitcase shut and she locked the two catches with a click. 'That's it,' she said. She rose from the floor and reached for her coat, sending the two boys ahead of her. 'We're on our way. Don't run into the street. Wait for me at the front gate.'

She followed them out and locked the door, putting the key in her bag. Her husband Mitek had been called up a week before the general mobilization and sent to the east. 'Don't worry, Soshka,' he had laughed, kissing her goodbye. 'The war won't last long. I'll be back in two or three weeks.' She had thrown her arms around his neck and wept silently. The train had whistled and given a lurch. Mitek had freed himself from her embrace and jumped into a carriage. Sofia had stopped running at the end of the platform, still waving her handkerchief.

I spotted her and the two boys as they were leaving the front gate. I moved away from the window and quickly began to get dressed. I wasn't affected by the general panic. The elder of her two boys was myself. I grabbed my coat and hat from the rack and caught up with them.

'Want a peanut?' I asked the smaller boy.

I thought perhaps he would hide his face in embarrassment. Or else reach out, take a nut, and crack it without a word. Say thank you to the man, his mother would surely tell him. But instead she simply looked through me, because I wasn't there.

'I'd like one too,' said the bigger boy.

How glad I am to see you here, I thought. But I didn't tell him that. And I thought: You're so small and thin. How strange to think that once your trousers actually fitted me. But I didn't tell him that either.

'Well, why don't you take one?' I held out the bag to him. He scooped up a handful of nuts. Some fell to the ground.

'Yurik!' scolded his mother. 'I asked you not to drag behind today.'

'I'm coming, mama. I just have to pick something up.'

Marisha opened the door for them.

'Boys!' she cried in surprise. 'Pani Doctor! Has something happened in Zoliboz?'

She relieved Sofia of the suitcase and helped her out of her coat.

'No,' answered Sofia, putting her hat on the table, 'nothing special. I just thought that we'd be better protected here in town. The children haven't eaten yet. Please give them some breakfast. And see to it they get washed. I'm going to lie down for a while. All I want is a glass of water.'

Sofia left the room and walked down the hallway. She went to her husband's office, rather than to his private room, and sat down at the desk. For a long time she let her fingers play with his array of rubber stamps hanging on their rack. She took one, breathed on it, and pressed it on the blotter in front of her.

> Dr M. M. Kosowolski
> 6 Graniczna Street
> Warsaw

'Pani Doctor?' Marisha was looking for her in the room across the hall.

Sofia stirred. 'I'm in here,' she said. 'You can leave the water on the table. I'll be right in.'

She heard the door creak and the saucer clatter on the glass tabletop as it was put down.

We're in luck that at least Marisha has stuck with us, she thought. I must tell her to oil the door hinges.

'Marisha,' she called after the retreating footsteps, 'please come in here for a minute. . . . I'd like you to oil the hinges of the door to the doctor's room when you get the chance.'

She smiled to herself halfway through her request, suddenly aware how ridiculous it was.

'Yes, Pani. I was just thinking the same thing myself. Do you feel any better?'

'Yes, a little, thank you. I'll take a pill and it will pass. How are the boys?'

'They're playing with the soldiers in the yard. They ate nearly everything.'

'If any more soldiers should ask to be quartered with us,' Sofia remembered to say, 'you can let them have the couches in the big room. There are some fine-looking boys among them,' she added with a smile.

'Oh, there are,' the girl agreed. 'One of them is the son of our neighbours in the village.'

Marisha left and Sofia rose from the desk and went to her husband's room. It was her favourite place. When the clinic bustled with nurses and silent patients filled the waiting-room she could always escape here from their curious glances. Through the shut door she could still hear the clacking of the typewriter and Mitek's calm voice, dictating.

For a moment she saw him standing there, or pacing across the room, pausing to look at the X-ray in his hand before continuing to dictate to the secretary.

She turned over on the couch and leaned her palm against the wall. How sturdy it was. The man who had made this house had built for posterity. The buildings in Zoliboz made her think of houses of cards that would be blown away by the first strong wind.

The doorbell rang. Sofia heard Marisha hurrying to answer it.

'Pani Doctor, old Pan Kosowolski is here.'

Grandfather Kosowolski! Sofia sat up and put on her shoes. Marisha was already hanging up his coat when she stepped out into the hall to greet him. Sofia liked her father-in-law. She especially liked his jovial face, with its fringe of a short, white, round beard.

'Hello, Sosha.' The old man embraced her and kissed both her cheeks.

Sofia took him by the arm and the two of them entered the dining-room.

'What will you have to eat, or would you like a drink?' She was happy to see him. 'Perhaps you'll stay here with us until everything blows over? How is grandmother?'

'She's fine, as usual,' he said. 'We have our daughter with us now, and the fact is,' he smiled, 'that I really did come to stay with you for a while. Perhaps I can be of some help. I'd planned to go to Zoliboz, but just to be on the safe side I thought I'd look in here first.'

Sofia sat him down in the easy chair. 'I'll call the boys. They'll want to say hello to you.'

She went to the window looking out on the yard and searched for them. Kazik was visible at once, sitting with a chubby soldier on one of the wagons and eating with him from the same mess tin.

'Kazhiu, come home. Grandfather's here.'

Such filthy utensils. God only knew what disease he might get from them.

'Kazhiu, come immediately. And call Yurik.'

She watched the little one clamber down the wagon wheel with the help of the soldier and head for the back of the yard. Only then did she spy Yurik. He was standing by a post to which horses were hitched, looking at them.

'Come on, Mama's calling us. Yurik! Did you hear me? Grandfather's here . . . Mama! He won't come.'

'Yurik,' called Sofia. 'Take your hands out of your pockets and come in. Grandfather's here.'

'In a minute.'

'Not in a minute, right now!' She shut the window with a bang.

A stubborn, wilful boy. Nothing matters to him.

She returned to the old man and sat on the arm of his easy chair.

'Don't think they're coming. I'll have to call them at least twice more. And it's always Yurik who's to blame.'

The old man patted her hand. 'How does he get on at school?' he asked.

'At school there's nothing but trouble,' she told him. 'All the boys hit him. He was lucky to get "satisfactory" for all his marks this year, except for conduct, of course, since he's always being hit. A month ago I discovered that he'd been giving his morning snack away to a boy from a higher class in return for protection. I went to the school and asked the children why they all picked on him. They said he was a creep. I told them that even if he was they should never hit anyone in the face. They said that when someone is so short it's the easiest place to hit him. You'll see him yourself in a minute. Most of the boys his age are a good head taller. And he's so pale. At least he's vomiting less now. I still can't travel on the bus with him, but a year ago he was throwing up after every meal.'

The old man burst out laughing. 'That doctor of his,

Meiner, or Meisner – what was his name? I once dropped in on you in the village when you weren't home. I went to the children's room and found the little fellow there, eating. He was eating very slowly, as though he couldn't stand what was on his plate. "What do you have there?" I asked him. "It's food," he said. "My lunch." I looked at my watch – it was three o'clock. I sat down next to him and said : " If you finish, I'll tell you a story." Five minutes went by, ten, twenty. "Well, why aren't you finished?" I asked. He shook his head and yelled : "Celina, a plate!" That Celina of yours came running, put a plate to his chin, and he threw everything up into it. The little devil just sat there, picked up his spoon, and began to eat it all over again. I was furious. But the girl tried to explain : "It's Doctor Meisner, his orders are for the boy to eat whatever he throws up." How many times had he thrown up already, I wanted to know. Three times, she said. And if he throws up again? Then he has to eat it again, she said. "Does Pani Doctor know about all this?" I asked. "Yes," she said, "it's she who says not to give in." Good lord, I thought to myself, how barbaric. But I didn't say anything.'

'It's the only thing that helped,' said Sofia. 'Here they come. What do you say, boys?'

'Hello, Grandfather!' they both said together.

'How are you, little fellow?' The old man stroked Kazik's face, then grabbed Yurik and pulled him between his legs. 'How are things at school, eh?'

Yurik shrugged.

'I've heard the boys hit you,' the old man continued. 'Because you're a creep, they say. Is that so? And don't you know how to fight back? It's every man for himself and never fear. Once, twice, you'll get yours, and the third time they'll get theirs. Then it'll be their turn to be afraid. What do you say?'

'You don't know anything, Grandfather,' Yurik said.

The village was spread out and spacious. It had thick woods and a stream to swim in. You could pick fruit and flowers and climb up the embankment of the railway tracks. The city was made of stone. The buildings were so tall that you could get dizzy from looking up at them. A lot of the streets looked the same, so that you couldn't find your way home without a grown-up. The city had cars, and carriages, and policemen, and the pavements were full of people. It had trolley-buses and show windows too, but the village was nicer. You could sit there and watch Francziszek the smith fixing leaky old pots, or play doctor with his daughters, or challenge Bogdan or little Zbishek who could pee further, or climb into a tree and count the carriages on a passing train. If it was a goods train you could count to a hundred or even more.

'Mama, will we ever visit Radosczi again? I want to go.'

'Of course we will,' she promised, but she never kept her word.

There were trains in Warsaw too. Travelling along the viaduct you saw lots of them down below, so many that they meant nothing and it was no fun counting the carriages of the passenger trains.

In Radosczi he had ridden a bicycle. Here, though, his mother didn't permit it. 'When you're a big boy.'

'But I've already ridden one, Mama!'

'How many times do I have to tell you?'

There were strange holidays here, too. There was the First of May, when you couldn't go out in the street. The red flag was nice to look at, especially at night, when it flew from the tall chimney of the factory lit up by an electric light. But he hadn't done well selling red balloons for his school. He sold three of them, one to an old man, one to a woman with a child, and one to himself, because he had ten cents left in his pocket. The other three flew away. He'd let go of the string and they'd soared high in the air. His mother hadn't wanted to give him the thirty cents for them. If you don't know how, don't volunteer.

'But they flew away!'

'Tell them that at school.'

He started to cry and she gave him the money.

In the school in Radoszi there were only six other children besides him, and the teacher, Pani Mueller. In Warsaw there were lots of children and they sat side by side at black desks. The teacher sat high up, on a stand. You had to raise your hand when you wanted anything or had a question. Sometimes you kept it up a long time and he still didn't see you. By now Yurik knew the way to school by himself. His first day there he had been brought by his mother, who had ushered him into class and left.

'What's your name?' the teacher asked.

'Yurik.'

A boy behind him laughed. The teacher looked up and the laugh was cut short.

'I mean your real name and your family name.'

Yurik understood. 'My name is Jerzy Henryk Kosowolski.'

'You can sit down.'

Then there was a bell and break. Two boys came up to him and asked : 'Are you a Yid?'

He shrugged his shoulders uncomprehendingly.

'You were asked a question.'

He opened his mouth.

'Go on, say something.' They began to laugh.

He shut his mouth without saying anything.

'Teacher's coming!' They pushed him aside and ran off.

The second lesson was better. The teacher read a story. Then there was another bell and another break. Two different boys approached him, one fat.

'Are you Catholic?'

'I don't know,' he said.

'You're not a Jew?' They were disappointed. 'Maybe just your mother's a Jew, or your father?'

'His name's Kosowolski,' said the fat boy. 'Jerzy.'

'Where do you live?'

'On a street.'

'What street?'

'A street that way.'

'We're asking you *what* street, idiot.'

'I don't know.'

'What *do* you know?'

'What?' Yurik didn't understand.

'Your father's moustache. Let's see your nose.' The fat boy grabbed him by the nose.

'Stop acting like a creep,' the boy sitting next to him advised him.

'I'm not,' said Yurik.

'I never saw such an idiot.' The boy made a face. 'Would you like a lollipop?'

Have a lollipop, darling. And he jabbed a pencil into his mouth.

There was another lesson. The teacher called on him and asked him to get up.

They all stared at him and tittered. He forgot the answer. Then he remembered, but he was afraid it wasn't right and they would laugh even more. He sat down. The bell rang and there was a long break.

'You don't know anything, Grandfather,' Yurik said.

'That's no way to talk,' said Sofia.

'Never mind,' the old man smiled. 'The young folk always know better, don't they? Well, go and play now. You've still time to learn from better teachers than me.'

Sirens wailed and the usual announcement came over the radio.

'Are you going down to the shelter?' asked the old man.

'No, we just step into the hallway in case of shrapnel. Come on in, children.' She sent them first and helped the old man move his easy chair.

The doorbell rang again.

'Marisha, answer it please. It must be the upstairs neighbours,' Sofia explained. 'Instead of going down to the shelter they prefer to duck in here.'

'If it's anyone with a suitcase,' she called after the girl, 'tell him to leave it by the door.'

There was quiet. The old man rested his head on the arm of the chair and shut his eyes. Sofia stood leaning against the wall.

'Sometimes they sound the sirens early,' she said. 'But sometimes they don't go off until the planes are already over the city. Please sit down,' she said to the newcomers. 'I'm sorry I can't entertain you in the living-room,' she joked. 'Marisha, we need another chair!'

There was a terrific explosion.

'That came pretty close,' said the old man.

'It must have been at number four.'

'*Oy vay, oy vayz mir,*' groaned one of the women.

'Yurik,' whispered Kazik. 'Look at that fat cow.'

'I can see her. She's an onion-stinking Jew.'

'Why is she shaking back and forth?'

'All Jews shake.'

'She looks like a witch. I wish she'd get out of here.'

19

'Shut up! Mama let her in. I heard her myself. Do you want to play something?'

'No. I don't feel like it.'

'Just remember, Kazik, I may not feel like it either when *you* want to. Let's play scratching airplanes.'

'All right,' the younger brother agreed.

'You haven't grown your fingernails specially long, have you?' Yurik asked suspiciously.

'No, look.' Kazik put out his hands and they compared fingernails.

'Let's go. But just with one hand.'

Another bomb fell close by. Sofia brushed the plaster that fell from the ceiling out of Kazik's curls.

'Mama, keep out of the way.' He pushed her hand aside.

'I'm not in the way,' she said fondly.

Another explosion shook the walls of the hall.

Sofia turned to the old man in the easy chair. 'I think perhaps we should go down to the shelter. I don't like the look of this bombardment.'

He rose energetically from the chair.

'Are we going down?' Sofia asked.

'Yes,' he said. 'Take the boys and start down. I'll follow in a minute.'

Sofia got the boys to their feet and went out with them, followed by the others in the hallway.

'Grandfather! What happened?'

'Jesus!' said Marisha in a fright. 'Pan Kosowolski is as white as a sheet.'

Sofia took his arm and sat him down on a stool. She took a bottle of valerian out of her purse and dripped a few drops from it onto a cube of sugar.

'Feel better now?' she asked anxiously when he had

eaten it.

'I'll be fine,' he promised, apologetic for being a nuisance. He tried to shake off the plaster that clung to him, but his hands wouldn't obey him. He crossed them on his knees.

'I had no idea they were already within artillery range,' he said. 'It's a lucky thing I have a second pair of glasses with me. I must have fallen on the ones I was wearing.'

Yurik and Kazik stood staring at him wide-eyed, their necks taut.

'How are you small fry managing?' he turned to them suddenly.

'Marisha,' said Sofia, 'I think I must have stuck my clothes-brush into the small valise. See if you can get it out of there. Pan Kosowolski's suit must be cleaned.'

The girl took the suitcase down from its shelf and stood it on a bench.

'Pani Doctor,' she broached the subject hesitantly, her head behind the open suitcase, 'that soldier, the neighbours' son . . .'

'You've already told me about him,' Sofia assisted her. 'What is it that you wanted to say?'

'If they pull out, he wants to take me with him.'

'I certainly won't prevent you,' Sofia said. 'I'll have to manage by myself for a while.'

She opened her purse and took out some notes. 'Not that you're going yet, but who knows? Here's for last month, and this is for . . . your wedding ring.' She smiled. 'You can take what you want of the children's old nappies. I think they're in the small room, in the top of the wardrobe.'

Sofia lay down on a broad wooden bench, her feet wrapped in a blanket.

'If it's quiet tonight,' she said, her head on a pillow, 'we'll all sleep upstairs in our beds.'

'Would you like another pillow?' asked Marisha.

'No, thank you.'

The kerosene lamps hanging from the brick walls cast a yellow light on the huddled figures in the shelter. The bombardment sounded deeper and further away now. Marisha covered Pan Kosowolski's knees with a blanket and began to knit.

'You'll ruin your eyes,' the old man said.

'It's all right,' she said, looking up from her knitting. ' What time is it now?'

The old man stuck his finger into his vest pocket and pulled out a large watch on a fob. He weighed it for a moment in his hand before releasing the catch on the cover.

'You know,' he said, 'this watch is twice as old as you are. It still remembers Odessa, Odessa from before the Revolution. Those were the days.'

Marisha sighed.

'Kazik, are you asleep?'

'No,' came the whispered answer.

'Ask the fat soldier to make me a leather whip too.'

Kazik didn't reply. Yurik turned to look at his brother's bed.

'Did you hear me?'

The darkness in the room wasn't thick. He could make out the dim silhouettes of the furniture and the white of the beds.

'Kazhiu,' he broke the silence again. 'Do you want to talk?'

'Yes,' Kazik whispered. 'But Mama will hear us.'

'She's sleeping far away,' his brother reassured him. 'Do you want my monkey to come over?'

22

Kazik hesitated. 'All right,' he finally agreed.

Yurik wrapped himself in a sheet and rolled out of bed.

'It'ssss me, the terrrrible, crrrruel monkey,' whispered the white shadow as it capered across the room.

'Why do you keep falling over?' Kazik asked worriedly.

Yurik stood up angrily: 'You're always ruining everything with your stupid questions. You're supposed to talk to me as though I were really a monkey.' He threw away the sheet and returned to his bed.

'From now on I will,' the little one promised. He looked at the floor of the room and asked anxiously: 'Did you leave the sheet on the ground?'

'Yes, there it is.'

'I can see it. It's white.'

'Listen. Do you want to play some more?'

'Yes,' Kazik said.

'Listen now.' From Yurik's bed came the rattle of a rhythmically shaken matchbox.

'Do you hear that? Those are my soldiers. They're getting into bed with me. Look how big my blanket has become.'

'Do they have horses?'

'Yes, but they left them below in the ground.'

'Did you see how the white horse died?'

'Yes. It had shrapnel in its stomach and its heart.'

'Can't horses be cured?'

'Papa could cure them.'

'No, he couldn't. He only cures people.'

'But he knows about horses too.'

'No he doesn't.'

'Yes he does.'

'No!'

'Yes!'

'No!'

They fell silent.

'No!' the smaller brother suddenly let out.

'I was thinking yes all the time,' said Yurik defensively. 'Did you see the man give me peanuts?'

'He gave me some too.'

'Mama said never to take anything from people in the street. They could be spies who give poisoned sweets.'

'Can you die from poison?'

'Yes.'

'You know, Yurik, I'm afraid of witches.'

'There aren't any witches.'

'Yes there are. They . . . they . . .'

'What are you whispering?' asked the older brother, alarmed. 'I can't hear you.'

'The witches.'

'Talk louder.'

'Mama will hear me.'

'No she won't.'

'Yurik, what's moving by the window?'

'That? That's the curtain. There's no such thing as ghosts.'

'Maybe there is. Is your sheet still on the floor?'

Yurik wrapped himself tightly in his blanket, careful not to leave a single crack. What if something should come out from under the bed and suddenly grab his foot? He wouldn't stick even his finger out from under the blanket now for all the money in the world. He kept his eyes on the white sheet. What was moving there by the window?

'Yurik,' Kazik whispered, 'I'm afraid. Maybe we should call Mama? I think they're already in the closet.'

'Who?'

'The pirates.'

'There aren't any pirates,' said Yurik. 'Be quiet and go to sleep.'

'Yurik, I have to pee,' Kazik whispered, choking back tears. 'I can't find the potty.'

'Did you look for it?'

'Yes.'

'Look again. Walk under the bed with your hand.'

Kazik groped along the floor with his hand. Yurik listened tensely.

'Well?'

'I can't find it.'

'Try again,' he encouraged him.

'I've found it,' Kazik announced.

'Are you finished?'

'Yes.' Kazik put the potty back down and curled up in bed.

'I have to go too,' Yurik groaned.

'Come on over.'

Kazik was clever, Yurik thought, he always kept the potty near him. What if something should come out from under the bed just now?

'Push it over towards me,' he said.

'It'll spill.'

'Push it slowly.'

Kazik looked with large eyes at the white, sheety animal that glistened in the middle of the room. He considered for a moment.

'All right,' he agreed. 'I'll push it over.'

'A little more,' Yurik begged.

'I can't.'

Yurik groped on the floor with his hand, but he still couldn't reach it. He crawled halfway out of bed, up to his knees.

'I've got it.' He breathed a sigh of relief.

'Let me have it back when you're finished,' Kazik asked.

'You won't need it again.'

'What if I do?'

'Then I'll leave it for you far away from my bed. Look, you can reach it easily.'

The clock chimed in the waiting-room. 'Twelve times,' Yurik counted.

'Kazhiu?'

From his brother's bed came the quiet, regular breathing of a sleeping child. Yurik turned to the wall and fell asleep.

A deer started on thin legs across a dirt road. He ran after it. The deer grew smaller, smaller and smaller.

The children were chasing him.

No, it was just a race. They didn't believe he could fly. Would he? His wings were so small. He didn't even have any. He pedalled furiously with his feet, soaring above the electricity cables.

'Did you see that?'

But they were gone.

An empty circus. He was the magician.

'Presto, horses!' Pairs of horses danced in front of him, alternately white and brown, their red saddles spangled with gold.

'Presto, a whip!'

He was a little afraid to try it, he didn't want to spoil the dream. But there it was! He pulled it from his pocket and slashed the air with it. The fat soldier could make a whip like that from the tiniest piece of leather.

He was sleeping now in the room where he had crawled on all fours as an infant. His parents had lived here before moving to Radoszci. His tattered monkey, with its human expression, on account of which his mother had bought it for him from a peddler, was still here.

How ridiculous grown-ups can be sometimes when a perfectly worthless object still has the power to fill them with obscure emotion. I went from room to room until I reached the waiting-room at the far end of the hallway. I explored each wall with my hands, each door.

Mama, open the door!

Mama, open it! Ma-ma!

Wait a minute, I'm busy. . . . What, crying already? I'll be there in a second. Such a cry-baby!

And later: Oho, I see you've already learned to bring a chair to stand on and open it yourself. Mitek! Come and see what this boy of yours is doing!

Did you ever think you'd have a chance to revisit the house in which you lived as a child? Did you still remember where to look for the hole in the corner in which lived the mouse who nibbled away under the floorboards at night? Were you disappointed when strangers opened the door?

Do come in, please.

Or did they look at you suspiciously and watch your hands to make sure you didn't steal anything?

Sofia took advantage of a quiet morning to visit her mother-in-law. The old woman opened the door for her, her sleeves rolled back and her hands dusty with flour.

'Good morning, Soshia. Watch out that you don't get all dirty.'

Sofia kissed her on the cheek. Was Stella home?

'Naturally,' said the old lady. 'She's still in bed.'

'I'll be right out,' called Stella from the next room. 'Just give me two minutes. How's Father?'

'Down in the shelter with the boys. He says he feels fine. Hurry,' Sofia added, 'the carriage is waiting.'

The old woman went back to the kitchen to knead her dough while Sofia chatted with her through the doorway. A photograph of Yurik when he was four hung on the wall. He was naked and holding a ball. Grandfather Kosowolski had pasted a paper leaf over his crotch. Sofia smiled. Yurik hated the picture, a duplicate of which was hanging in her bedroom. It embarrasses me, he told her. There's nothing to be embarrassed about, she had answered. Why aren't you embarrassed by your nose, or your hand?

'Take it down. It embarrasses me.'

'You're just a little sillyhead.'

'I'm warning you, I'll steal it and throw it out the window.'

Stella finished dressing and came into the room. 'That was quick, wasn't it? I take it we're going to the bank.' A new suit, tailored to match her tall body and dark complexion, peeped out from beneath her fur coat.

'Bye-bye, Mother,' she said to the old lady. 'If there's an air raid, be brave and go down to the shelter.'

The two women left the house and got into the waiting carriage.

'Have you shut your shop?' Sofia asked.

'Yes, but the girls are still sewing. They say that after the war there'll be a great demand for women's hats.'

Stella owned a fancy hat store. She had built it up all by herself and was proud of her independence.

'You'll never get married,' Sofia had once predicted of her darkly. 'All those generals of yours aren't worth a damn.'

Nevertheless, Stella had married a young businessman from Lvov a year ago. Yurik and Kazik had a new uncle.

'Do you have any idea where he's stationed?'

'Yes,' Stella said. 'I forgot to tell you. A friend of his stopped by. They're dug in somewhere near Warsaw. He wouldn't tell me where. They love to have their military secrets, those men.'

On their way back from the bank they were surprised by a siren. They took cover in a gateway together with the carriage.

'Oh, how I hate that wailing,' said Sofia, hunching her shoulders.

The old coachman looked up at the blue sky.

'All I need is for them to drop a bomb on my Ruzhinka now, those sons of bitches.' He clapped his hand to his mouth and added : 'I beg your pardon, ladies.' The two women smiled.

'Actually, I'm supposed to unharness her,' he said, recalling the safety regulations. He stepped out of the gateway.

'Hey, what are you doing out there?' shouted a steel-helmeted policeman.

'Yes sir, officer, right away, I'm just giving my horse some food.'

The raid went on for two hours. Sofia was worried about the children. When the all-clear sounded she decided to go straight home.

'I'll see you soon. Love to Mother.'

She opened her purse and handed the coachman a coin. 'Don't bother,' she said when he reached into his pocket for change.

'Thank you, madam, you're very generous.' He whipped the reins and shouted : 'Giddy-up, Ruzhinka !'

Stella reclined on the upholstered back seat and listened to the rumble of the wagon wheels and the clip-clop of the horse's hooves on the cobblestoned street.

'It's a lovely day today,' she said.

'Lovely is the word,' said the coachman. He lit a cigarette and looked at her out of the corner of his eye. Jewish or not? He wasn't sure.

'That's a nice horse you have,' she said.

'Ha!' he laughed. 'When you wash 'em and scrub 'em and put a ribbon in their tail, why shouldn't they look nice?'

She speaks like a fine lady, he considered. Who was to say?

'God grant that this war be over soon,' he said.

'God grant it,' she repeated.

It wasn't any proof. The Jews had a God too. He squinted at her again and shrugged.

'Number forty-two,' he said, stopping the carriage. He jumped down from the driver's seat and helped her get out, hoping for a tip. Stella took a coin from her purse. 'This is for you,' she said.

He bowed. 'Many thanks, madam. You're most generous.'

She stepped up to the horse and caressed its thin nostrils.

'I see you like horses.'

'Yes,' she giggled. 'Do you have a piece of sugar?'

The old driver fumbled in his pocket. 'I swear, it's a sin to spoil 'em in times like these,' he said, producing a filthy cube.

Stella took off her glove and gave it to the horse. The driver climbed back up on his seat.

'Goodbye now.'

'Have a nice day,' she said to him.

The horse gave a lurch and pulled the carriage after it. The coachman looked back at Stella's shapely frame and the long fox-stole draped around her shoulders. A real good-looker. What the hell! Giddy-up, Ruzhinka, let's get on home. The old lady is waiting for us.

'Grandfather?'

'What is it, Kazhiu?'

'Mama's still not home.'

'Don't worry, she'll come soon. Come and play horsy on my knees.'

The old man took out his watch. She'd been gone for three hours. She should have been back by now.

A loud explosion shook the walls of the shelter. The shock waves blew open the door and extinguished all the lights.

'It's dark!' the little boy wailed.

The old man didn't answer him. He lit a match with unsteady hands. Marisha gave him a candle. Someone came in the door and shut it.

'Mama!' cried Kazik.

She hugged her two children and sat down next to them. 'You see, your mother came back. She always does. Were you crying, Kazhiula?'

'No.'

'He was,' Yurik said.

'They were both perfectly fine,' the old man put in.

Sofia stood up and took two chocolate bars from the suitcase. 'One for each of you,' she said.

Evening came. A strange silence hung over the city. A soldier in full battle dress came into the shelter.

'Marishka, we're moving out, are you ready? Good evening, Pani Doctor,' he said to Sofia.

'Has something happened?' she asked anxiously.

'They say the whole city's in flames. They've been dropping nothing but incendiary bombs since early afternoon.' He bent down to take the girl's suitcase. Marisha said goodbye to Sofia and the boys and kissed the old man's hand. Soon after there was the sound of wagon wheels and hoofbeats. The soldiers were leaving the yard.

'The whole quarter is on fire!' the civil defence leader of the house came to inform them. 'The Saski Gardens are burning too. We've got orders to evacuate while we can.'

Everyone rose heavily from his place near the walls and began packing his belongings. Sofia gave Kazik his coat and helped him find the sleeves. Yurik wore a beret. They left the shelter and went back up to their apartment. It was dark. The house was deserted. An insidious noise, like the crackling of wood in a stove, came from the street. Sparks flew in the air. The window panes shone with a leaden colour.

'Hurry up,' Sofia urged them. 'Everyone's in the street already.'

She threw a few more things into the small suitcase and took the children's hands. The old man lingered in the hallway.

'Are we leaving everything behind?'

Sofia didn't answer. 'We're the last ones out,' she said at last. 'We have to be quick.'

'I'm taking the two suitcases of winter clothes,' he decided, bending down to pick them up.

Sofia looked at him in astonishment. 'Father, are you out of your mind? It's not worth getting killed for a few old rags. Put them down and come.'

The old man held on to the suitcases. 'Let's go,' he said.

They went down to the yard. Near the front gate Sofia noticed a blonde girl hiding under the stairwell.

'Come with us,' she said, running over to her. 'You can't stay here by yourself. Come along,' she prodded. 'You can't stay here.'

The girl wouldn't budge. 'I'm waiting for my mother,' she sobbed.

'Your mother's already where we're going,' Sofia assured her, trying to take her hand. The girl slipped away and ran towards the gate leading to the second yard in the rear.

'You'll never find her in the dark,' the old man called to Sofia.

Sofia hesitated. Flames glowed near the gate. She quickly took the children's hands and they left. A crowd of people blocked their way.

'You can't get through!' they shouted. 'Go back!'

'Mama,' complained Kazik, 'I've got smoke in my eyes.'

'We'll be out of here in a minute, son, just hang on.'

A spark fell on Kazik's coat and caught fire with a little flame. Sofia saw it in time and brushed it away. The old man couldn't keep up. Sofia looked back and opened her mouth, but she didn't say anything.

The houses on both sides of the street were burning and thick smoke covered the sky. It kept getting hotter. Behind them they heard a building crumble and collapse.

My God, don't let one fall on us, Sofia whispered. The street was littered with belongings thrown away by the fleeing crowds.

I stopped short. They kept walking and I followed them with my eyes.

Was it all perhaps only a fairy tale? There they are, walking on, amid the tall buildings and the flames, growing smaller and smaller until they disappear right out of the picture. The tiny silhouette of an old man in a top hat moves cumbersomely down the cobblestoned street between two mighty columns of flame that join together in the burning sky, dragging two suitcases in his hands.

33

2

'Is the war over, Mama?'

'It is for the time being, Joasia.'

'Where are you going?'

'To look for your Aunt Soshia and her two boys.'

'I'm coming too.'

'No, Yoasha, you stay here.'

The girl puckered her lips and prepared to cry.

'What if Papa should come home and not find anyone here?'

Yoasha loved her father so much that for his sake she was even ready to stay at home by herself.

'All right,' she agreed.

'Don't tease the cat and don't open the door to strangers,' Anna warned her. She bent to kiss her daughter.

'Come home soon, Mama. 'Cause maybe Papa will come.'

Anna waved to her from the stairs and smiled. She knew perfectly well that her husband wouldn't be coming home today or tomorrow. He had been sent like Sofia's husband to the eastern front, where no doubt both had already been taken prisoner by the Russians. She would have to take care of the children and run his X-ray clinic by herself until the war was over. Anna had graduated from medical school a year after her husband, and both of them, she and Sofia, had met their future husbands on the same day. Anna was younger than Sofia and prettier. In her home town she had been thought the local beauty. Of the whole large family, the two sisters alone had moved to Warsaw, where they had grown very close. Yurik and Yoasha were born in the same month, and since Anna refused to nurse her baby, Sofia had taken her sister's child and nursed her too.

'You and your figure! You're a model mother.' Soshka the saint, Anna had thought. The two children grew up. Yoasha remained an only child, bossy and spoiled. Yurik became Yurik.

A band of unarmed Polish soldiers straggled wearily down the middle of the street, wrapped in their winter army coats. They were being demobilized. Armed policemen tried to restore a semblance of order to the capital. Carcasses of horses, stripped of their edible meat, lay about the streets. Anna reached the ruined quarter where her sister lived. It wasn't easy to find Sofia's house. The street looked totally different. A policeman showed her the way. She found and entered the yard. The house was still smouldering. She hurried out. By the front gate her eye was caught by the shod foot of a child sticking out from under the rubble. She took off her coat and began to dig away at the pile of burnt bricks. She heaved a sigh of relief when she saw the shock of blonde hair on the girl's head. She pointed out the corpse to the policeman on the street and ran home.

'Mama,' Yoasha greeted her, 'Aunt Sofia and the boys are here!'

Anna struggled free of her embrace and ran to the back room.

'Soshia! Why didn't you let me know you were safe? I've just been to look for you.'

The sisters hugged each other in a long embrace.

'Some strangers put us up overnight,' Sofia said. 'Plain, decent people. You know, the little one's begun to grind his teeth at night. I think it must be from all the bombing.'

'Yoasha, are you asleep?'

'No.'

35

'Talk to me.'

'Do you like dogs?'

'Yes.'

'I like cats better. Before the other half of our house was destroyed, the neighbours' dog used to howl all night. You know, like wolves at the moon. Did you ever read about them? Mama wanted to adopt him after they were killed, but he wouldn't let us take him.'

'Maybe I can adopt him?'

'He won't let you. Sometimes dogs just lie down on their masters' graves and die there from hunger and sorrow.'

'Did you ever see one?'

'What a dope! When they're dead they get thrown away.'

'I'd have it buried next to me,' said Yurik.

'You're not allowed to,' said Yoasha. 'Cemeteries are only for people.'

'But what if a bird fell in one and died?'

'Sshhh, my mother's coming.'

Anna opened the door. 'Yoashka, if you don't stop talking we'll have to separate you.'

'All right, Mama.'

'Good night.'

'Good night, Mama.'

'Yoasha,' whispered Yurik.

'Not yet. Wait till she's gone.'

'Who do you like most, your mother or your father?'

'My father,' said Yoasha. 'I love walking with him in the street.' She got out of bed and went to get one of her dolls. 'We'll play in whispers,' she said.

The siege lifted and the surrender terms were signed. Rescue teams searched through the debris for people who were buried alive. Sanitation workers began to clear the ruins. After the tension of the air raids, the artillery bombardments, and the fear of gas attacks, there was a feeling of relief. Sofia returned with the two boys to Zoliboz. Their house was untouched. She opened the door and let out a deep breath.

The German army passed through Zoliboz in a big parade : swords, drums and crisp uniforms. No one stopped to look at them. The children peeked out at them on the sly.

Winter came. Occupying soldiers strolled along the streets among the passers-by. If asked their opinion, they would politely but confidently declare that soon they would rule all of Europe.

'As far as the Urals, would you say?'

There were some citizens of the former Polish Republic who cast in their lot with the conquerors. Their motives were various. With some it was a matter of background or politics, with others it was belief in a German victory. sometimes it was simply fear, or poverty, or not having enough coal to burn. You wouldn't believe that the gentleman walking past you now on the street carried an identity card stamped *Jude*. Strange how you couldn't tell by the face.

'By the Holy Trinity,' said Marek.
'We swear.'
'By your father and mother.'
'We swear.'
'By the honour of a Pole.'
'We swear.'
'By the white eagle and the flag.'
'We swear.'
'In the name of the fatherland.'
'We swear.'

37

'By the Gospels.'

'We swear.'

'That's all,' said Marek. 'Any *Volksdeutsch* that we discover will go on the black list. Don't forget to keep the secret. Whoever tells gets flogged. What about you?' he turned to Yurik.

'What about me?' Yurik asked, surprised.

'You can't swear by the Holy Trinity or by the Gospels either.'

He stood there bewildered. I believe in Jesus, he wanted to tell them, but he was embarrassed.

'They have the Old Testament,' someone said. 'And he can swear by God. The Jews have only one.'

Marek consented. 'Now by yourself,' he said.

'By God.'

'By God,' Yurik repeated. 'I swear.'

'By the Old Testament of the Jews.'

'I swear.'

'Our motto is : *Death to all traitors*. Blow out the candle and we'll stand at attention for a minute in honour of our country's fallen heroes.'

When they left the cellar the stars were already twinkling in the sky.

'Let's try number eighteen,' suggested Bolek. Yurik agreed. They entered the strange yard and climbed up the stairs.

'Are you scared?'

'No. Who lives here?'

'I think just the sister of the shopkeeper on the corner.'

'Ring the bell.'

Yurik pressed the button. They heard someone approaching the door. As long as it's not a man, Yurik thought. A woman opened it.

'Whore!' Bolek shouted at her and the two of them

ran down the stairs, ringing all the doorbells on the way.

They reached the safety of the street.

'That was good,' said Bolek, slapping Yurik on the shoulder. Bolek was his hero. He had once accidentally set off a grenade and nearly got himself killed. Yurik snitched cigarettes for him from his aunt and Bolek let him smoke one. Bolek could blow smoke from his nose.

They met two other boys on the way. The four of them walked along making plans for the next day.

'How did you get on?'

'We called her a whore and ran. It was terrific.'

They parted by the front gate. Yurik went home. He met his brother on the staircase. Kazik stood there with his legs wide apart and didn't move.

'What's the matter?' Kazik didn't answer. Beneath him was a puddle. 'You wet your pants, that's what. Mama! Ma-ma!'

Sofia opened the door. 'What is it?' she asked anxiously.

'He went in his pants,' Yurik announced. 'He just stands there without moving. He's cuckoo.'

Sofia came down and took the little one by the hand.

'Come, Kazhiula, let's go upstairs. Don't pay your nasty brother any attention. You come up too, Yurik!'

Yurik came upstairs and waited.

'I told you to come up because I wanted to talk to you. Look here, Yurik. I'm not going to scold you or spank you. I just want you to tell me the truth. Was it you who took the cigarette papers from Aunt Stella's purse?'

'Yes,' he said.

'And you've been smoking cigarettes?'

'Yes,' he confessed.

'I want you to promise me never to do it again.'

'I promise,' he said. 'Can I go down now?'

'It's too late. Your supper will be ready in half an hour.'

Because of the fuel shortage, Sofia had shut down most of the rooms in the apartment for the winter. The beds were all moved to the room near the kitchen. At Christmas time she received a letter from her husband, from the Russian-occupied sector of Poland. Other letters followed. Mitek wrote that he was working in a hospital and lacked nothing. In one letter he hinted that she should try to join him by illegally crossing the border. She refused. The winter was severe and she was afraid to endanger the children. She decided to wait out the war in Warsaw.

Anna's husband wrote too, from a detention camp in Hungary. Stella's husband, Vilek, returned home right after the surrender of Warsaw.

For the first time Sofia didn't buy a fir tree for Christmas. Yurik went to the tree market and brought back a small shrub that someone gave him for nothing. That afternoon he stood in a church, his hand in the palm of an old, wrinkled beggar woman. Both stared enchanted at the pictures of the manger in which the Christ child was born.

'Look, here's the infant Christ. And the holy mother is happy, so happy. The whole world has come to bow down to him, because he's the Messiah. He so loved innocent children.'

'Did the saints really have light like that around their heads?'

The half-deaf old woman didn't hear. She kept fingering her rosary and whispering prayers. Yurik stood on tiptoe and shouted into her ear : 'That light around their heads, was it really like that?'

'Of course,' she assured him, nodding her head. 'Just like that. They were saints.'

Yurik! What are you doing here?

Praying.

You've run away from home?

He nodded. Grandmother grabbed all my soldiers from the table. She gets cross when anyone says that it's good that Papa was an officer and fought for us.

Oh, I said.

She's Jewish, Yurik added.

Aren't you too?

I'll become a Christian when I grow up.

'Jewish, Jewish,' the old lady mimicked the boy. 'What a darling boy. Would the gentleman believe it? I was taking him around the church, and suddenly he says to me : "You know, Pani, I'm a Jew." Pani, he calls me. Ha ha ha!' She bared her toothless gums. 'A Jew he wants to be yet!' She bent to shake a bony finger at him. 'The Jews are bad. They crucified our Lord. They kidnap children in the street. Yes, they do, yes, they do.'

'Would the gentleman like one?' She offered me a postcard of the Virgin. I gave her ten cents.

'God bless you,' she thanked me.

I left the church with the boy. Go on home, I told him.

Grandmother will spank me.

No, she won't, I reassured him. She's over it by now.

He wasn't listening to me any more. He had his face up and his mouth wide open, trying to swallow one of the falling snow flakes. Then he spread his legs wide to keep his balance and followed the flying flakes round and round as they plunged to the earth, as far as the eye could see.

Go on home, she's over it by now, I said again.

He went. A frozen puddle was in his path. He took a running start and slid across it on his heels. Then there was a second puddle, and a third, too, but not as big as before.

3

Spring came. The snow ran off into the gutters and the pavements were dried by the sun. The occupation authorities had not been idle. After issuing a decree forbidding Jewish children to attend Polish schools, they published a second one ordering their parents to wear a white armband with a blue Star of David on it. A deadline was set for prohibiting Jews from venturing out of the ghetto.

'Is just your father a Jew?'

Yurik kept silent.

'Because your mother never wears the armband. It's your turn.'

Yurik kneeled and flicked his chestnut into the hole. They began a new game.

'Ah, I don't feel like playing,' Yurik said.

'Come over to our place,' suggested Tadek. 'My mother will give us a snack.'

Yurik agreed. They gathered up the chestnuts and went. Tadek was considered one of the toughest boys in the neighbourhood. Yurik couldn't remember when they had become friends. Maybe it had been on that day when someone had shoved him in the street?

'Move, scum!'

'Leave him alone,' Tadek intervened. 'I said leave him alone.'

'I didn't think . . . I mean I didn't know . . . that you were with that Jew . . . that you were his friend,' the boy corrected himself.

Yes, it had probably been on that day. They walked together down the street. Neither said anything. They stuck their hands in their pockets and went from one shop window to another.

'I'd really like a bicycle.'

'I was promised one this summer,' said Tadek.

'Shall we go to Kraszinski Park afterwards?'

'Okay,' agreed Tadek. 'How's your football team?'

'My goalie broke. You know the one. The big red button.'

They turned in at a gate and climbed the stairs. Yurik liked to visit his friend's home. Tadek's father worked for the post office. He delivered mail. He had a uniform and a bicycle.

Tadek knocked on the door. 'It's us, Mama.'

A small, neatly combed woman let them in. 'You're just in time. The kettle's boiling. I'll make you some tea.'

'Drink up,' she encouraged Yurik, as though he were an honoured guest. 'Do you make trouble for your mother like he does?' she asked with a smile. 'Do you hitch rides on the back of trolley-buses, too? They caught him in the end, and did he get it at the police station!'

'It didn't hurt,' Tadek said. 'They spanked me through my pants.'

They drank the tea and ate biscuits. Then they got up. 'We're going now, Mama.'

'Have a good time. And don't get into any scrapes in the street.'

'We won't. We're going to the park.'

Yurik liked Tadek's mother. Apart from his own family, which didn't count, he had already had several loves in his life. First had come Celina's Edward. The one in the fire department. He had loved her other Edward too, who was the bodyguard of the rich lunatic who lived in the woods. Celina had still a third Edward, the village letter carrier, whom he didn't love. Celina herself wasn't eligible for the love list because she had always been part of the family. But Helenka the maid was. She was always chasing him out of the kitchen. You fat arse, he said to her once. He knew another dirty word about women, but he hadn't said it. He didn't like Helenka. After her came Tekla. Tekla was undoubtedly a saint, or at least half of one. They always waited for the nights when the three of them would be by themselves, and Tekla would put them to bed and tell stories. Yurik swore to her he would become a Catholic. And he would, no matter what. He didn't like Miss Yanka. She was Jewish and ugly. After Celina's marriage and Miss Yanka's arrival to take her place, the soldiers in the park had stopped playing with them. Celina had married Marian. It's types like him that get all the best girls, Yurik's mother had said. Then they had a son whose name was Robert.

The biggest of his loves, though, was Jan, the doorman at the sanatorium. Jan had a green uniform. Yurik drew a heart with an arrow in it on a paper napkin and gave it to Jan early one morning as he was sweeping the stairs with a long-handled broom.

Kraszinski Park was green with spring foliage. The boys strolled several times around one of the fountains and sat down to rest on a bench. A toddler in a white suit was jumping up and down nearby, playing at something.

'He's got terrific buttons,' Yurik whispered to Tadek.

They eyed the benches. A girl was sitting not far from them, next to a policeman. The policeman had his arms around her and her head was in his lap.

'You think he's hers?'

'She's the only one around.'

'Hey pal,' Tadek called. 'Would you like a penknife? Come on over here for a minute.'

The child stopped playing and stared at them.

'A real penknife,' Tadek promised him, swinging his legs on the bench.

The child approached them uncertainly and stared at Tadek's hand.

'Here,' said Tadek, handing it to him. The child was dumbstruck. He had never dreamt of such a miracle.

'Peneye,' he gurgled, grabbing it in his fist. Meanwhile Yurik was at work on his suit, stripping off the buttons that were usable for football with quick turns of his hand. 'Finished,' he announced excitedly.

Tadek snatched back the penknife and the two of them dashed off. The little boy screamed like a siren.

'What's wrong, darling?' His frightened governess dashed over to him.

'Peneye,' he wailed. 'Peneye.'

'Jesus!' screamed the girl. 'All his buttons!'

Tadek and Yurik were already far from the park.

'One's got a belly,' said Yurik.

'You can file it down on a wall,' Tadek observed professionally.

A trolley-bus passed by, ringing its bell.

'What do you say?'

'Not today,' said Tadek. 'I don't feel like it. Come on, I'll show you the hole with the horse.'

They crossed the trolley tracks and headed for the last row of houses in the neighbourhood.

'Over there,' Tadek pointed.

They came to the edge of a pit.

'It's a hole,' Yurik said.

'It must have been some bomb.'

'Is it a horse?' asked Yurik.

'The head looks like a horse's,' said Tadek, 'Everyone says it's a horse.' He picked up a stone and threw it at the carcass. Yurik found more stones and threw them too.

'Use bigger ones. You won't even break one bone with those.'

'It's strong,' Yurik marvelled. 'It must have been a dray.'

Tadek scratched his head, tilting his cap. 'It's no go,' he said. 'Maybe we should just roll a big rock down.'

They began rolling one, manoeuvring it towards the edge of the pit.

'Let 'er go!' cried Tadek.

The rock crashed down by itself. It shattered the top of the horse's skull, so that the mouth grated open. Tadek and Yurik ran off. They stopped far away, panting heavily.

'It talked,' whispered Yurik.

'Perhaps the devil was in it?'

'I have to go to my lesson,' Yurik remembered.

'Don't you go to school?'

'No.'

'Why not?'

'I just don't.'

'Where do you have your lessons?'

'With Pani Landau. Together with Rishek.'

'Rishek the kindergarten teacher's son?'

'Yes,' said Yurik.

Tadek threw a glance at the pit. 'Come on, let's go around it,' he suggested. They made a long detour and parted.

Rishek opened the door for him. 'We've got a plan!' he shouted, hopping on his foot that was in plaster. 'Listen, it's fantastic. Come on.' He pulled Yurik to his room, relieving him of his books on the way.

Rishek's friend Hippolyt was standing in front of the closet, taking out its shelves and the bricks that supported them.

46

'He'll hide inside during the lesson,' Rishek explained in a fever. 'Go look out the window and see if she's coming.'

Yurik climbed on the window sill. 'I can't see her,' he said.

'Hippolyt's taking the giraffe with him,' Rishek explained. 'He'll signal to us with it through the glass. Got it?'

Yurik got it. 'Here she comes,' he called, jumping down from the window.

Rishek locked the closet door and stuck the keys in his pocket.

'Okay,' called Hippolyt from inside

'If I cough, that means chickie,' Rishek reminded him.

Yurik went to open the door.

'Good afternoon, boys,' said their teacher.

'Good afternoon,' the two of them answered.

She pulled up a chair and sat down. 'Have you prepared all your lessons?'

They burst out laughing, got hold of themselves, and then started laughing again. Just then Hippolyt did a dance with the giraffe on the glass door of the closet.

This time they laughed so hard they couldn't even try to hide it.

'You've caught the giggles?' she asked. 'Very well, I'll give you five minutes to get over them.' She opened her newspaper and began to read.

They looked at each other, but it wasn't funny any more. Hippolyt was quiet in the closet. Then he coughed.

'That must be the sick neighbour,' said Rishek. 'He just coughs all day long. And at night he doesn't let us sleep.'

'Maybe he's got TB,' said Yurik.

'There he goes again,' said Rishek.

The 'neighbour' suddenly toppled over.

'Open the closet,' said Pani Landau.

'My mother locked it.'

'Look in your pockets for the key,' she said.

'I really didn't know I had it,' Rishek apologized, pulling the key out of his pocket. He opened the side of the closet with the hangers. It didn't occur to Pani Landau to look where the shelves were. She looked in the next room but found nothing there.

The lesson lasted two hours.

'Goodbye children.'

'Goodbye, Pani Landau.'

'Has she gone?'

'Yes. You can open it now.'

Rishek opened the closet door. Hippolyt fell out.

'Yurik, open the window,' Rishek yelled. 'Fan him with a towel.'

Rishek took the giraffe and returned it to his sister's cupboard. 'What's the big idea?'

'My goddamn legs fell asleep. I thought you'd never finish your shitty lesson. I was about to choke in there.'

'Tomorrow we'll hide you in the bed,' Rishek promised.

'She's coming back,' Yurik whispered.

'Crawl under the bed,' Rishek ordered. 'And you, shut the window. Hurry!'

'It's me,' said Pani Landau. 'I'm back. I wondered if you might be so kind as to introduce me to your neighbour?'

'What neighbour?' asked Rishek.

She smiled. 'Next time don't leave Hippolyt's shoes in the hall. Don't forget to do your homework for tomorrow. Bye-bye.'

'Fooey!' spat Rishek when she'd left. 'Yurik, take a rag and clean up what I just did.'

'I don't want to,' said Yurik.

Rishek stepped up to him and swung back his plaster leg. 'Goddamn it, did I tell you to do something or not?'

Yurik tried to escape, but Hippolyt grabbed him by the leg.

'I'm not wiping it up,' Yurik whined.

'All right, don't cry,' Rishek said. 'Just go and get me a rag.'

Yurik took his books and left. Rishek had no father. He was alive, but Rishek didn't know where. He didn't even know if his father was Catholic or not. His mother was Catholic. Perhaps his father was a Jew? What would that make Rishek? Half-and-half, Yurik guessed.

The gang from number eighteen jumped him in the street and grabbed his hat.

'Officer,' cried Yurik, 'they took my hat.'

'Give him back his hat, you rascals.'

They threw him the hat and ran off.

What are you crying for?

They took my hat, Yurik sobbed. He tugged at his nose, then wiped it on his sleeve.

Wipe your nose with a handkerchief, I said.

He took it from me, blew in it, and handed it back.

Are you going to cry some more?

No, he gasped.

Come on, I'll buy you a sheet of soldiers to cut out.

Big or small? he asked.

Big, I promised.

We crossed the avenue.

It's here, he said, pointing at the toyshop.

Which do you want – the firemen, maybe?

He looked at me suspiciously. You said a big sheet of cavalry!

Right you are, I forgot. Cavalry? All right, then, cavalry.

I bought it for him and we left the shop. Where were you coming from just now? I asked him.

We had a lesson, he said.

Was it interesting?

I don't remember, he said. Did you know, he said, they killed my grandfather.

I stopped short. What are you talking about? When?

Oh, a long time ago. He was frightened by my alarm. They did it because the Jews killed a soldier near our house.

It had happened in the spring, I recalled. The snow was already running off into the sewers. A lot of bodies could be identified and buried after the weather thawed. Stella came to identify her father's. She looked at one corpse after another as the workmen pulled them from the muck. She stopped by the last one. She bent down, and I could see a gold chain in her hand, at the end of which hung a large pocket watch.

Is that him?

Yes. They dragged him away.

She opened her purse and paid the workmen.

Yurik walked away from me down the street, immersed in the galloping soldiers on the paper sheet.

Towards the end of that summer, the day before the sealing of the ghetto, in which all the Jews now had to live, Sofia passed out through the yard of their house carrying a knapsack on her shoulder. This time she put on her white armband on the stairs, and not, as she usually did, on the trolley-bus on her way into town.

Kazik walked beside her, clinging to her arm. Yurik lingered behind, carrying a three-masted boat.

'Yurik, why can't you keep up with us?'

'I'm walking,' he replied. He was a little embarrassed to have to pass through the yard so close to a Jewish mother.

4

Out of my way, boy! The man was fat as a pig. Already begging money for cigarettes at your age, eh?

Another man stopped and searched in his wallet.

Here, this is for you.

A couple passed next to me. Should I let him have something? she asked. Look, you can see he's from a good family.

The boy put out his hand. Be kind to a poor, starving boy, madam, be kind!

Once you start giving, he said, there won't be any end to it.

Oh, come, darling, just this once.

I waited until they were gone and put a gold half-crown in his hand. Yurik looked up.

Did your mother put you up to this?

He shook his head.

Then who did?

They're doing it too.

Who?

Those girls from Wlicov Street.

Are they friends of yours?

Yurik didn't answer.

I know you don't have girlfriends. I know you hate girls. Do you really mean to tell me they're your friends?

Yes, but . . .

Where are they?

Over there, he pointed.

Wait for me, I told him. I'll be right back.

A few houses around the corner I ran into two girls his age, holding collection boxes for the Poor Fund. I returned to him.

Look here, I said, they're collecting for the Poor Fund. What about you?

I'm collecting for him.

Oh, I said.

Not far away sat a boy dressed in rags, swaying back and forth to the hoarse rhythm of his cry : 'Have mercy, a piece of bread, have mercy. . . .' His face was yellow, like an old man's, and he wore a tattered brimmed hat on his head. His legs were tucked under him from the cold.

Him?

Yes, said Yurik.

You . . . I began to say and then stopped. I didn't know what to say.

Well, I have to run along now. Goodbye.

Goodbye.

Please, sir, he reached out his hand to a man in a leather coat. It's for a poor child, sir.

Yurik stopped by the toyshop and pressed his face to the window pane. On a glass shelf inside was a row of Indians riding lead horses. One after another they bounded frozen in their daring jumps, in their hands a lasso, bow-and-arrow, or rifle pointed at the white conqueror's heart.

Yurik bent over to see them better from the side. Looking up from under the horses' hooves, it seemed to him he could see not dozens, but thousands, of mounted riders. You could see an endless row of Indians, especially if you squinted a little.

'Hey you, get your filthy hands off my window!'

He leaped back from the glass pane and looked the proprietor in the doorway up and down with blazing eyes. He wandered off.

No one can catch me, he thought, overtaking one person after another in the street.

'Excuse me, sir, do you have the time?'

His lesson was due to start in ten minutes. He still had time to get there. He lingered on the wide steps of the courthouse, looking at the ornamentation on the columns : an axe and grape vines, just like the Romans'. If only he could find some little Roman soldiers, ones that were really alive. A whole tiny city of them, with houses, and horses. The things he could do with all that.

A man in torn clothes reached into Yurik's pocket and lifted out the paper bag containing his morning snack. Two men passing by came to the boy's aid. One held the pickpocket by the collar while the other hit him in the face. The man didn't try to defend himself. He simply turned his head to one side and hurriedly crammed the bread into his bulging cheeks. He fell onto the steps on his back, crumbs of white cheese all over his coat. His assailants let him lie there. One of them came over to Yurik.

'Don't let it worry you, son. But next time keep an eye out. Don't walk around with your head in the clouds when there's bread sticking out of your pocket.'

Yurik ran off without thanking them. Whenever he saw anyone being hit, he got a strange lump in his throat. He thought about the man who had stolen his bread. You could swallow paper, but what had he done with the string it was tied with? He reached into his pocket and out it came, a piece of wrapping twine.

53

Yoasha opened the door.

'Pani Landau's already here,' she told him. 'You're late again.'

'So what?'

'Let's see if you tell her "so what" too.'

'Someone swiped my sandwich from my pocket. Is Aunt Anna home?'

'Yes, my mother's in the X-ray room.'

Yurik knocked on the door. 'Aunt Anna, this is from Mama.' He handed her a package. He took his jacket and returned to Yoasha's room. 'Someone swiped my sandwich,' he repeated defensively.

Ever since he'd come under Pani Landau's wing, Yurik had begun to learn. Sometimes he'd still get one of his 'black-outs', as she called them, when he couldn't grasp the simplest arithmetic exercise, but they were much less frequent. Yoasha was quicker to catch on than he, but once he understood something, he never forgot it again.

'I know *Marathon* by heart.'

'It's about time,' said Pani Landau. 'Up to where?'

'All of it,' he boasted.

'Really? Get up and let's hear it. Wait a minute,' she stopped him, 'what's that in your mouth?'

'Oh, nothing.' He spat out the chewed string and stuck it in his pocket.

' "Sardis is in flames," ' he declaimed. It excited him, and the words flowed vibrantly. Pani Landau was pleased.

'I can see you decided to make my last lesson a memorable one,' she praised him. 'Has your mother told you yet?'

'She hasn't told me anything.'

'But I know,' Yoasha volunteered. 'You're crossing to the Polish side. And we'll get a new teacher.'

Pani Landau smiled. The little girl knew everything. 'Come, let's drink some farewell tea.'

Yoasha jumped down from her chair and opened the dining-room door. Anna invited them all to sit down. 'You sit here,' she said to Yurik. Yurik sat down and picked up a saccharine pill.

'Look,' he nudged his cousin, holding it above his cup, 'it's about to fight for its life.'

'You've told me that joke at least twenty times.' Her answer slighted him. He reached out and pulled her braid. 'Aunt Anna, let me sweeten your tea,' he said to Yoasha's mother.

'It's our second war,' said Anna to Pani Landau. 'The first was much better. We had a German officer billeted with us who gave us German lessons. We still thought of them then as a decent, civilized people. And now . . . another cup of tea, Pani Landau? By the way, did I ever tell you? A day or two after the surrender two German soldiers came by, put a gun to my head, and asked for money. I told them in Polish that they might as well get it over with and shoot, since they weren't going to get a cent. They turned around and walked right out.'

'They said Mama was brave,' Yoasha put in.

'I wouldn't have dared risk it,' said Pani Landau. She rose from the table and shook Anna's hand. 'I've got to be off. Adieu,' she said to the children. 'Let's shake hands. We won't see each other again till after the war. Try to be good students of whom I needn't be ashamed. Especially you.'

Yurik nodded. 'Goodbye,' he said.

The two women left the room.

'Draw some more,' he requested Yoasha. 'Let's go on with the story.'

'Go and get some paper,' she said. 'I've got a pencil here. The paper's in the desk drawer.'

55

Yurik brought paper. Yoasha began to draw the sorcerer.

'You've left out a foot,' said Yurik.

'It doesn't matter, I'm drawing his brother.'

She drew Tom Thumb walking on stilts to raise himself to a normal height, Pinocchio with his dog, and the Pied Piper.

'Here, let me. I'll draw the Jews and the rats, and you draw the boy and the girl.'

From the street came a hoarse, repeated cry: *'Alle gleich! Alle gleich! Alle gleich!'*

'It's crazy Bronstein,' Yoasha shouted happily.

The two children dropped everything and ran to the window to see him.

On his way home Yurik decided to visit his Aunt Mania. If I ever own a shop, he thought, it'll be a bakery. He pushed open the door and walked in. A bell tinkled. His aunt was busy putting little cakes in a cardboard box.

'Here you are.' She handed the package to a customer. 'Yurik,' she exclaimed, seeing him. 'How are you? Come over here, I have something for you.'

He stood by the counter and followed her hand with his eyes. Would it be a piece of cheesecake? Or a brownie? Or perhaps. . . . She gave him a brownie. Then she took three more little cakes and wrapped them up.

'Here. Take these to your mother and give her my best. And be careful no one grabs them on the way.'

Yurik tucked the package under his jacket and left. Now he was an automobile. He slipped expertly in and out among the people on the street, dodging a thousand fatal accidents in his path. He was a small car, a racing car. The big cars all had blue armbands on their arms but not him. He was like the Poles. When his automobile reached Lesznau Street he decided to play policemen. As far as Stella's house. Each bar on a policeman's sleeve was one point. When he got to Stella's house the other side of the street was winning. Too bad. Perhaps tomorrow his side would win. He went through the gate and up to the second floor.

'Hello, Yurikle.' His grandmother was happy to see him. 'Come on in, would you like some cake? I'll give you a piece.'

'Don't give him anything,' called Stella from the next room. 'Afterwards he won't want to eat lunch and Soshia will be upset. Come over here to your aunt, you little devil,' she called to him.

Yurik went into her room and sat on the side of her bed.

'Are you sick?'

'No. Don't you know that your aunt loves to lie in bed? I can't think of a nicer thing to do. Take off your jacket, it's hot in here.'

Yurik took off his jacket. 'Blow smoke rings,' he asked.

She drew heavily on the cigarette and blew out a series of rings. They widened as they rose, gradually losing their form, until they finally vanished somewhere near the ceiling. Yurik followed them intently.

'More,' he begged.

'What's in that package?'

'Cakes.'

'Were you at Aunt Mania's?'

'Yes,' he said. 'Tell me about the foxes.'

'But I've already told you twenty times.'

'I don't care. Tell me again.'

'I had a fox coat,' she said. 'I came to visit you. You were standing in the room and you stared at it.'

'I was a little boy then,' he reminded her.

'Yes, you were little. You asked me: do they bark? I said yes. Make them bark, you said. I barked. And then

57

you threw up all over the floor.'

Yurik smiled. 'More,' he begged. 'About the telephone.'

'But you know that one too.'

'Tell it,' he insisted.

'We were talking on the telephone,' she began impatiently.

'We made it out of matchboxes,' he reminded her.

'Yes, you were just a little tot then. Hello, hello, who's on the line? This is the director of the zoo, here. And who are you? Yurik, you said. Hello, hello? This is Yurik. That's all you knew how to say on the phone then. Finally I got tired of it and said : This is the doctor here, are you sick? Yes, you said. What seems to be the matter? I asked. I have a stomach ache, you said. I'll be over right away to give you an enema, I said.'

'And I threw up.' Yurik laughed gaily.

'What's so funny?' she smiled.

'Go on, tell me something else,' he said.

She took a cigarette from her packet and lit it. 'I see you remembered that you had an old aunt who told stories.'

Stella told him about their séances, and about the cat that scared Aunt Mania out of her wits. Yurik listened to her greedily. Stella glanced at her watch. 'It's time for me to go,' she told him. 'To this day she believes that she saw a ghost on the stairs.' She grew serious. 'It sounds funny, but once I had a dream about someone that really turned out to be true. I had a friend who promised me she wouldn't go and see a certain man. That night I dreamt that I saw her stopping by his house in a sled with a bouquet of red flowers, dressed in a blue gown. And that's exactly what she did. The flowers she brought him were actually red and her gown was blue. What do you think of that?'

Yurik didn't answer.

58

'You'd better be off. You'll be late for your lunch and your mother will be cross. Come, give your Aunt Stella a kiss.' She pulled his head towards her and kissed him on the mouth. 'Wait, I'll wipe off the lipstick.'

'What, you're going already, *mein kind?*' the old lady complained. 'So soon? Here, this is for you.' She opened her purse and gave him a coin.

'Don't give it to him for a rickshaw ride,' called Stella from her room. 'He has two healthy legs to walk on.'

'I'm not, I'm not,' said the old lady. 'On your way now,' she whispered, pressing the coin into his palm.

Yurik was back in the street. He put the coin away for tomorrow.

On his way home he paused on the wooden bridge that crossed a Polish street bisecting the ghetto and, leaning against the railing, looked down.

A red trolley-bus went by. Then a car. Three children were returning from school with their briefcases. A woman and her son entered a shop. Two men stepped out of a carriage drawn by a white horse and approached the checkpoint at the ghetto gate directly beneath the bridge. The Polish policeman checked their papers and let them pass. They must be important people, he thought.

Some Jewish policemen closed off the street to Polish traffic. Now a Jewish street swarmed beneath the bridge. Large numbers of rickshaws went by. Tomorrow he would ride one to school. Just like that woman down there, the one with the hat. She was wearing silk stockings too. He would sit like a king. Too bad he wasn't really a king. Kings drank tea through straws made of sugar.

Yurik descended from the bridge, counting the steps. At its foot a new shop had opened. He read the sign : THE BOTTOM OF THE BRIDGE CAFÉ.

Two children were selling Star-of-David armbands by the

display window. They had linen bands with the star embroidered in blue, and elegantly shiny cardboard ones covered with celluloid. The cardboard ones cost more. His mother had the simpler kind.

'Finest armbands!' cried the girl.

'Strongest armbands!' cried the boy.

A pale woman with heavily rouged lips was standing by the entrance to the house, the kind you weren't supposed to talk to. Yurik went upstairs.

'Hello Mama.'

'Hello son. Is everything all right?'

'Yes,' he said. 'I smell smoke,' he sniffed.

'I've had another hard day today,' she said. 'But the food isn't burned. Nissim is eating with us today.'

'Nissim from the front of the house?'

'Yes,' she said. 'Not all the children are as well off as you.'

'This is from Aunt Mania.' He put the package on the table.

'Thank her for me the next time you see her. You must have gone to scrounge from her, mister big-eyes.'

'Mama, what are the notes on all the doors?'

'Lists of tenants,' she explained. 'It's a new regulation.'

Yurik opened the door and began to read out loud : '1. Sofia Kosowolska. 2. Yurik Kosowolski. Why does it say Yurik and not Jerzy?'

'So they'll know you're just a boy and won't come to take you away to work. Close the door. It's cold.'

'3. Kazhiu Kosowolski. 4. Stanislawa Panska. 5. Wanda Panska.'

He shut the door with a bang when he was finished.

'Don't you know better than that?' she asked, annoyed. 'Open it again and shut it quietly.'

'Mama, Alle Gleich didn't die like you said he did. We

60

saw him running in the street today.'

'I'm happy to hear that.'

'What does *alle gleich* mean?'

' "Everyone is equal." '

'Why does he go around shouting it?'

'Because he's crazy.'

'Then everyone isn't equal?'

'That's enough. Don't you ever know when to stop? When we die we're all equal.'

'Why are you happy that he isn't dead? Why should you care about him?'

'It's sad when anyone dies.'

'Even Hitler?'

Sofia didn't answer.

'Mama, you know, I went begging.'

'Is that in a story you wrote?'

'No. I really begged. For the boy next door.'

She put down the knife she was holding and looked at him.

'You begged for money on the street?'

Yurik took fright. 'Just a little. For half an hour maybe.'

'Holy mother!' she moaned. 'They'll say I sent you out to do it. Doctor Kosowolski's son. You've gone out of your mind!' she shouted. 'Where were you begging?'

'On Krochmalna Street.'

She grabbed him and held him by the shoulders.

'Did you see anyone we know?'

'I don't remember.'

'Try to!' She shook him. 'Exercise your brain a little.'

'I don't remember,' he said. 'I didn't see anyone.'

She let go of him and returned to the stove. 'You can drive a person crazy. Don't you ever dare do it again, do you hear me?'

'Yes.'

'You promise?'

'Yes.'

'Here, here's half-a-crown. Give it to the boy when you go downstairs. Don't forget. God knows what I'll do with you.'

'All right,' he promised.

'I don't need you standing around here in all this smoke. Go to your room.'

He left the kitchen and went to Pani Panska's room. Little two-year-old Wanda was sitting in her cot. Yurik went over and stuck his hands between the bars.

'Wanda, Wanda,' he called to her, wiggling his fingers.

She pulled herself up by the bars, smiling at him.

'Say Yurik,' he told her. 'Go on, say it.'

'Ek, ek,' she babbled happily, sticking her fist in her mouth.

Sofia was proud of their new apartment. Not everyone who was forced to move to the ghetto had three rooms and a kitchen. She had got it through the offices of the Zoliboz Corporation, which had been given her old apartment in return.

'The management there arranged for you to get this place? There are some good *goyim* too.'

'There are good people,' Sofia corrected. She didn't like the word *goyim*.

The rooms of her new apartment were small, and were set off from each other by a step, but she still had two of them to herself. The third room she had given to Pani Panska. Stanislawa worked in a nursery school. Before the war she had been a violinist in a symphony orchestra. She earned next to nothing now, and had nothing of any value left to sell. From time to time she sold blood to the hospital, and used the money to buy extra food for her daughter.

'Don't overdo it, it's doing you no good,' Sofia warned her.

Stanislawa smiled. 'What else can I do?'

Her husband, an infantry officer, was listed among the dead at Katyn. Yurik and Kazik liked their tall, thin lodger, especially when she told them stories or played for them on her violin.

'Yurik, perhaps you'd like to feed the little one? Pani Panska seems to be late today.'

'All right. But just to feed her.'

'I've already put her on the potty,' she reassured him.

Yurik put the infant in her highchair and sat across from her with a bowl of cereal.

'Open your mouth,' he said. 'A little more, that's it.' He slipped the spoon into her mouth and let the cereal slide off.

There was a knock at the front door.

'Yes, Kazhiula, I'm coming. How was school today? You didn't hit anyone?'

'No,' he said. 'I got a "very good" in arithmetic.'

Sofia bent down to kiss his forehead. 'Take off your coat, Kazik.'

Kazik went into Pani Panska's room.

'I want to feed her too!'

'It's my turn now,' Yurik insisted.

'Let me give her just one spoonful.'

'No, get out of here.'

The younger brother remembered something and ran off to the kitchen.

'Mama,' he said, 'you know what, I saw a louse on the stairs! It just stood there and looked at me. A real louse.'

Sofia inspected his jacket. 'Are you careful not to bump into people in the street?'

'Yes,' he said.

'Go on inside, and don't stand here in all this smoke.'
She chased him out of the kitchen. 'Your lunch will be
ready in a minute. We're eating early today, because I've
got some washing to do.'

Yurik finished feeding the infant and wiped her face
with a towel.

'Mama, I've finished. I'm leaving her in the chair.'

Kazik came out of the kitchen and the two of them
went to their room.

'Let's play war-on-the-step.'

'I don't want to,' Kazik said. He reconsidered. 'All right.'

He put down his books and stood on the step, his back
against the dresses and coats hanging on the door, ready for
the attack.

'For God and for country!' cried Yurik. 'Up and at
them!'

'Long live Poland!'

The older brother charged forward, trying to get up on
the step.

'No hitting!'

'I just pushed.'

Yurik backed off to the end of the room and charged
again.

'The fort will hold out to the last drop of blood,'
Kazik whispered through clenched teeth.

The hanger broke and all the clothes fell on their heads.
They immediately came to their senses.

'You did it.'

'No, I didn't.'

'Let's try to fix it before Mama comes.'

'Lunch is ready!' called Sofia from the next room.

They didn't answer. They stood waiting to see what
would happen. Sofia tried to open the door.

'Didn't you hear what I said? What's in the way there?

All the coats and dresses! Oh, my Lord!'

'Stella! Come on in, but shut the door behind you so that the smoke doesn't get out. I'll be with you in a minute.'
Sofia took off her apron, glad to have her work interrupted.
'How are you? I see you're smoking like a chimney again.'
Stella sat on the couch and blew smoke at the ceiling. 'They've arrested Vilek,' she said. 'Someone informed on him yesterday while he was on the Polish side. I had a feeling it was going to end this way. It must have been that debtor of his. Now there'll be no more debts.'
The two women sat talking quietly. Sofia received a small monthly allowance as the wife of an officer in the reserves. No, the children didn't know about it. How much longer would she still have belongings to sell? And then what? Stella was moving in with a certain Pan G. Who could he be?
'Someone with connections,' said Stella without further comment.
The front door opened.
'Pani Panska?'
'Yes, it's me,' said Stanislawa.
'Come on in. Join us for tea.'
Stanislawa came into the room. 'May I? Brrrr, it's cold out there.'
She sat by the table with her small daughter on her knees. 'Don't touch anything,' she warned her.
Sofia poured her some tea. 'You don't look well today,' she said. 'Have you taken your temperature?'
Stanislawa sipped her tea, pressing her hands against the cup to warm them.

'No. I feel fine.'

'I haven't heard from Mitek at all,' Sofia said to Stella. 'Perhaps I was wrong not to have tried to cross over last year. But it was a hard winter, and to think of having to smuggle myself across the border with two children. . . . Boys, be quiet in there!'

'They're such babies,' said Stella. 'The older one especially.'

'Let them be. The more babyish these days, the better.'

'Thank you for the tea,' said Stanislawa. 'I have to put Wanda to bed for her nap.'

'It's time for me to go too,' Stella reminded herself.

Sofia walked her to the door. 'This Pan G. – perhaps he can help you somehow with Vilek?'

'I've already thought of that,' said Stella. 'I'll try him.'

Sofia shut the door after her and returned to the kitchen.

It was already four o'clock. Tomorrow she had to go to pick up her allowance. She put a flat bowl beside the basin and transferred the rinsed clothes to it. She'd rather stand here all day washing than have to go for the money. The street, the children begging for bread, the corpses covered with newspapers, the long lines of women, the roughness of the Jewish policemen – it was all too much for her. It was almost Yurik's birthday. He was eleven already. What could she possibly get him? Mickiewicz's poems? What might they cost these days?

'Mama!'

'What's wrong?'

The two children burst into the kitchen in a fright. 'Mama, it's Pani Panska!'

Sofia wiped her hands and rushed into the next room.

'She was playing the violin for us,' said Yurik, 'and then. . . .'

Stanislawa lay moaning on her bed.

'Stanislawa, what is it?' Sofia bent over her.

Stanislawa sat up a little and laughed contortedly.

'Jesus, she's gone mad! Kazhiu,' said Sofia, 'get dressed and go and call her mother-in-law. You know where she lives, on Chlodna Street. Why are you so pale, son?' She caressed his face. 'It's nothing at all, she's just been taken ill. Be quick now, and be careful in the street. You, Yurik! Take a rickshaw and go and get Aunt Anna from the hospital.'

Sofia scribbled a few words on a piece of paper and handed it to him. 'Take some money. Make sure you don't lose the note.'

'Should I come back in a rickshaw too?'

'All right, come back in one too. But hurry.'

The two boys went out. Stanislawa began to mutter something and then let out a scream. Sofia took the bawling baby to her room. God in heaven, why should the children have to suffer?

Kazik was back with old Pani Panska in half an hour.

'Why must you live five flights up!' she complained. 'What's wrong with Stanislawa?'

Sofia helped her out of her coat. 'She suddenly took sick,' she said, trying to prepare her gradually.

The old lady went to Stanislawa's room and sat down next to her. Stanislawa opened her eyes.

'You!' She sprang to her feet and grabbed her mother-in-law by the throat.

Sofia rushed to the old lady's aid and broke Stanislawa's grip.

'Go to my room,' she told the mother-in-law, who was in a state of collapse.

Stanislawa clung to Sofia's hands, trembling all over. 'Stay with me, Pani Doctor,' she pleaded. 'I'm so scared.'

Anna and Yurik arrived in an ambulance. Placidly,

Stanislawa went down to it. Sofia sighed with relief.

'How many times did I tell her not to sell her blood!' she said to the old woman. 'As soon as she came home today I saw she didn't look well. But she'll recover quickly,' she added encouragingly. 'Shall I send Yurik along with you?'

'No, thank you,' said Stanislawa's mother-in-law. 'I'll take her a few things to the hospital and go home. It's not far from here.'

Sofia sat on the window sill. Outside it was getting dark. A large pile of garbage rose in the middle of the square courtyard. Boys chased each other. Two little girls were playing hopscotch to one side.

Sofia spotted Yurik and Kazik trying to climb up the drainpipe. She opened the window and called:

'Boys come inside. It's time for supper, Yurik! Kazhiuuuu!'

Light trickled through the blackout paper on the window in the boys' room. She would have to do something about it. The day before yesterday she had practically broken a leg in the unlit street. It had been pitch dark. She still felt sore on one side. If it wasn't for the new phosphorus pins that people wore on their clothes, they would constantly be colliding with each other. Yurik had already managed to lose his pin. She wouldn't buy him a new one. Let him learn a lesson. Sofia ran her finger over the window pane in a long spiralling line, drawing rings within rings. She pulled herself away from the window and went back to the kitchen.

The boys came in panting and ran straight to their room.

'Yurik,' she called, 'I'd like you to chop me some wood. I've got nothing left to put in the stove.'

Yurik came back with wood.

'Here's branches for kindling, Mama. Two bundles of a

hundred. You owe me twenty more cents.'

'Fine,' she said. 'Put them down by the stove.'

'Will you read to us from *The Magic Journey* today?'

'If you wash by yourselves I will.'

'Tell me, has Pani Panska gone mad for the rest of her life?'

'No. She'll be better soon and then she'll come back.'

Yurik took the axe and went out into the corridor.

'Watch out for your hands,' she called after him.

She left the plates on the table after dinner. She'd done enough for one day, she decided.

'Go and wash,' she said, chasing the children from their room. 'Who's first tonight?'

'All right, I'll go first,' Yurik offered magnanimously. 'But read to us.'

He began to undress while Sofia opened the book.

'Do you remember where we're up to?' She read slowly, stopping now and then to explain the hard parts. Suddenly she looked up from the book and smiled at Yurik. 'Don't forget that you're in the middle of washing,' she said to him.

Yurik snapped out of his trance and went on soaping himself. If only he could become Thumbkin, flying through the air with the wild geese.

'Mama, dry my hair,' he requested.

Sofia put down the book and reached for a towel. The boy laid his head in her lap. Something cold suddenly touched his back. He whirled around and knocked a glass out of Kazik's hand. It shattered on the floor.

'He touched me with a cold glass.'

'It wasn't on purpose,' Kazik defended himself.

Sofia looked from one to the other.

'Can't you see,' she said carefully, 'that Kazik was trying to surprise me by drying the dishes?'

Yurik became angry.

'You always take his side. You did yesterday too when he wouldn't take off my shoes. You just don't understand that when he loses a bet he has to carry out my orders.'

'All right,' she said. 'I'll sweep up the pieces myself. If you don't stop quarrelling, I'm not going to read any more.'

They quietened down. Sofia finished drying Yurik's hair and gave him a comb.

'Here, comb it yourself.'

The fire was getting low in the stove. The children listened to the magic story, huddled against their mother.

'And now good night.' She kissed each boy on the cheek and closed the door behind her. Now the room was dark, except for the scant rays of light that passed through the cracks of the door.

'Do you want to tell stories?'

'You tell one,' said Kazik.

Yurik thought for a moment. 'You know,' he began, 'I've built myself a castle under the sea. . . .'

Sofia counted what little money she had left. I won't touch the jewellery yet, she decided. I'll keep it for harder times. Her brother Edek was bound to arrive in Warsaw from Lvov any day now. When he came, he would sleep with Yurik, and Kazik would move to her room. Everyone knew him in Lvov; having missed his chance to go east with the Russians, it was best for him to at least leave the city. Her father wanted the whole family to come and stay with him in Czestochow. Should she agree? But she didn't want to leave Anna, and Anna couldn't leave her clinic. So the two of them had better stay in Warsaw. The war couldn't go on forever. She heard the two boys whispering in the next room. She tried to listen. The older one was a strange boy. What would become of him? She was sorry she had hit him yesterday. But he had simply driven her crazy. She had to control herself more. She reached out and switched off the electric light.

The boys were still whispering.

'Crazy Bronstein ran and I ran after him,' said Yurik. 'He jumps into a carriage and I jump after him. He lets the man have it in the face, then the woman, then the driver, and then he jumps out the other side. So I let them all have it too, bam, and jump out after him.'

'You're not afraid?' marvelled Kazik.

'No, he knows how to make me very strong.'

'Where did he get all those eggs from?'

'I bought them for him. We made a huge omelette. This German came down the street – and Bronstein grabbed him and threw him into the omelette. Then we spat on him.'

'How long have you been his friend?'

'Always. He just pretends he's mad. He's a big magician and he isn't afraid of anyone.'

'Can Pani Panska come here if she wants?'

'No.'

'Yurik, when we're giants, how big will we be?'

'We'll get bigger and smaller as we like.'

'Will we take Aunt Mania with us?'

Yurik thought it over. 'Yes,' he decided. 'She's our aunt. We'll take Uncle Sokol too, and Pani Panska. We can take them all in our pockets. And then we'll escape from the ghetto.'

Kazik fell asleep. Yurik lay there still half-awake.

Yurik Yurik Yurik. It came with a melody from far away.

He mustn't answer. The old woman in the church told him that. It was Death calling.

The melody came nearer. Yurik Yurik, he heard it whispering beneath the windows with the voices of many people. Now they were calling to him from very close. He froze under his blanket, trying not to breathe.

He was travelling in a rickshaw through the streets of Vienna. The houses were white cubes.

The telephone rang. Sofia went over to it and picked up the receiver.

Hello? Hello? Who's speaking?

This is Sverdlovsk. Pani Doctor Kosowolska? This is Sverdlovsk.

Speaking, she said excitedly into the phone.

The voice faded for a moment, then came clearly again.

Your husband is alive. He's in Sverdlovsk. Did you get that? Sverdlovsk.

I hear you. My husband is alive. Hello? Hello? But the connection was already cut off.

Sofia woke up and flicked the light switch. The electricity was off. Where had she left the matches? She got out of bed and walked barefoot to the table. She lit a candle with shaking hands. Sverdlovsk? Was there really such a place? She pulled down an atlas from Yurik's shelf and leafed through it feverishly.

Suzdal . . .

Suva . . .

Svendborg . . .

Sverdlovsk . . . there it was. A large city in the Urals. Could it be that she had really never heard of it? Yes. She was prepared to swear to it. Sofia smoothed out the map and bent over it by candlelight. The black dot grew bigger, became a metropolis. What was he doing there? What a strange dream! She shut the atlas and blew out the light. A small spark at the tip of the wick still smouldered for a while in the darkness, but it too went out before she could get back into bed.

The Lvov-Warsaw train is nearing the capital. Three men bounce back and forth in it to the oscillating rhythm of the carriage. All three are wearing fur jackets and boots. The one in the middle has closed his eyes and leaned his head back against the seat. Who would dare to approach these three brawny workmen sharing a bench to ask them for their papers?

The middle one, if you ask me, is actually not so broad-shouldered. He's on the short side, too. Watch it! You mustn't point as you walk down the aisle. He's a Communist.

Would Pan Engineer care for a cigarette?

Edek roused himself. Thank you, he said. Have we still far to go?

Another half an hour at most.

Open his jacket and reach into the inner pocket of his vest, there you'll find a glass vial whose label says: Cyanide! Danger! Poisonous!

Yurik reached out for the wall but didn't find anything there. He groped on his other side and encountered it. The room spun around and returned to itself. Yurik readjusted the blanket, turned over the pillow, and lay down on its cold side. He thought he heard knocking at the front gate. He listened for a moment.

'Uncle?'

Edek woke up. 'What is it, Yurik?'

The door opened and Sofia came in, lacing up her nightgown.

'Edek? Get up and get dressed. There's a search on.'

Heavy footsteps echoed in the yard. Edek jumped out of bed.

'Hurry up. I'll bring you your jacket.' She paused to listen in the darkness. 'They're coming up here. Yurik, make your uncle's bed. Cover it with something.'

Edek slipped into his jacket and crawled out onto the balcony. Sofia locked the door behind him, pushed a table against it with the boys' help, and readjusted the blackout paper. 'Get back into bed,' she told them.

The steps approached the door of their apartment. They passed it. The fists of the soldiers hammered on the door of the apartment across the hall. 'Who is it?' asked a frightened woman. Then they heard a key turn in a lock, shouts, someone running on the stairs, a shot.

It was a starless night.

The soldiers threw the old father of the man who had tried to escape out the window. After him they threw an upholstered armchair, so that he might have something to sit on while complaining to his God.

Yurik woke up again. The house was quiet. He opened his eyes and saw Edek kneeling on the window sill.

'What are you doing, Uncle?' he asked, scared.

'Nothing, Yurik,' said Edek, shutting the window. 'Try to sleep.'

Yurik turned over towards the wall. He must fall asleep before his uncle began to snore. Should he count to a thousand? No, elephants were better. They put you to sleep faster.

One elephant and one elephant were two elephants. Two elephants and one elephant were three elephants. Three elephants and one elephant were four elephants. Elephants. A whole herd of elephants.

'Here goes!' yelled Yurik. He threw a handful of postage stamps into the air.

The two of them leaned out of the open window, following the stamps as they fluttered down over the yard. A group of boys below waited for them to land.

'They're reaching the ground!' shouted Kazik excitedly.

The boys fell on the treasure, fighting for it furiously. Soon there was a pile of bodies on the pavement of the courtyard. They got up and straightened their clothes. Two or three sneaked a glance to see if their stamps were still in one piece.

'Did you see that?' asked Yurik enthusiastically. 'I'm going to throw some more.' He searched through the envelope of doubles, but there were only five stamps left in it. 'Hand me the album,' he ordered Kazik.

'Yurik,' called his mother. 'Someone's at the door. Go and see who it is.'

'Just a minute.' He turned to his brother. 'Kazik, go and open the door. That's an order. I have three orders left.'

'You won't throw them while I'm gone?'

'Even if I do, there's still lots more in the album. If you don't go right now, I'll never play anything with you again.'

'He's not your servant,' Sofia intervened from the next room. 'Don't go, Kazhiula. I told Yurik to open the door.'

Yurik went to open it. He let in a tall man in a blue suit.

'Good morning,' said the man. 'Is Pani Doctor Kosowolska at home?'

'Please come in,' said Sofia warily. 'I'm she. Whom have I the honour of speaking with?'

He introduced himself and smiled.

'Please have a seat. Yurik, bring our visitor a chair. What can I . . .' She didn't go on. 'Do you have any news of . . . my husband?'

'Yes,' he said. 'I was together with Doctor Kosowolski in

the prison at Brisk. They jailed him for illegally trying to cross the border back to you.'

'Just a minute,' Sofia said. 'I'll bring you some tea and something to eat. You must be hungry.'

She went to the kitchen and pressed her palms against her forehead. God in heaven! She put the kettle on and returned.

'Kazhiula, come in here,' she called. 'What a shame that Edek isn't here. He went to ghetto headquarters to propose a new invention for making artificial honey. He's an engineer,' she explained. 'Come and introduce yourselves, boys.'

Her eldest stepped forward. 'Jerzy Henryk Kosowolski.' He put out his hand. Kazik was too embarrassed.

'It's all right, sit down. Our visitor has brought us news about Papa.'

The boys sat next to each other on their mother's bed. The visitor told his tale. Sofia forgot all about the water boiling in the kitchen. Her face flushed with emotion. She saw her husband playing chess with pieces made out of bread, sewing slippers for himself out of an old blanket, settling arguments between the prisoners. My Mitek!

'Who won?' Yurik wanted to know.

'Generally your father,' said the visitor, laughing and pinching the boy's cheek. 'I'm not very good at chess.'

'The tea!' Sofia remembered. 'Perhaps you'll stay a while longer?' she asked.

'I can't,' he apologized. 'I have to get back to the Polish side today.'

Sofia accompanied him to the door and walked with him to the street.

'I can't tell you how grateful I am,' she murmured, when he kissed her hand. 'The best of luck to you.'

'Where's Yurik?' she asked his brother when she was back upstairs.

'He went out,' said Kazik. 'I'll bet to one of his girl-friends.'

'The fool,' she grumbled. She sat Kazik on her knees and he put his arms around her neck. 'You see, Kazhiula, Papa's alive. We'll see him again after the war, and then we'll be ever so happy.'

'Mama.'

'Yes.'

'Yesterday a German officer gave out rolls to poor children in the street.'

'You're imagining things again,' she smiled.

'No, really. He had a big basket. Ask Yurik.'

'Maybe he did,' said Sofia. 'Today I'll believe anything.'

Summer came. The penniless survivors sighed with relief. The typhus epidemic eased a little. The soldiers shot into the air, or among the passers-by, to laugh at their panicky flight.

Sofia dressed and went out with her two boys to visit her sister on Yoasha's birthday. On the corner near their house sat a jaundiced-looking boy with a broad-brimmed man's hat on his head. 'Have mercy,' he said. 'A piece of bread. Have mercy.'

'Kazhiula, take a penny and give it to the boy.'

5

The electricity went off and Sofia lit a candle and put it on the table. Several of the neighbours had gathered in her kitchen. Among them were the woman who lived in the apartment across the hall, the laundress and her husband from upstairs, the vegetable dealer who lived right above them, the grocer from down below, and Nissim from the front gate, who had happened by on some errand. Yurik and Kazik got out of bed and sat by their mother, next to the stove.

'What do you think, Pani Doctor? They say we're all going to be deported from here.'

Yurik watched the large silhouettes tremble on the wall with each flicker of the candle flame.

'I've heard that in a number of towns the Jews have all been taken out to the forests and shot.'

'That's ridiculous,' objected the grocer.

'They say,' said the neighbour from across the hall, whose husband and father had been killed in one night, 'that they'll murder us all.'

The laundress's husband began to laugh. 'What are you talking about? Half a million people? Women and children too? It's unthinkable. The whole world will rise in protest. There's still such a thing as public opinion. There's still England and America.'

His wife agreed with him. 'Next you'll be saying they'll kill all three million Jews in Poland!'

'Maybe it's true about the small towns,' her husband continued. 'But this is a city, and a big one. There's the Polish working class and the underground to be reckoned with.'

'Don't talk to me about the Poles,' the vegetable dealer snorted. 'If they help anyone in the end, it will be the Nazis.'

'There's really just no knowing,' said the woman from across the hall.

'They say,' said the grocer, 'that we're going to be evacuated from the Little Ghetto, as far as the bridge.'

'What, from here?' asked the woman from across the hall.

Sofia held her two children tight and said nothing. The candle flame flickered and the silhouettes shook. The woman from across the hall kept wringing her hands. Nissim fell asleep, his elbows on the table, supporting his head.

'The poor boy,' said Sofia. She rose, gathered her two children, and put them back to bed.

'Where are we going?'

'To somebody's apartment. Aunt Stella lives with him.'

'Are we leaving our books and toys here?'

'For the time being,' said Sofia. 'Say goodbye to your uncle, he's staying here.'

Edek bent to kiss them. Then he embraced his sister.

'Be careful, Edek,' she begged him. 'I hope Pan G. will let you come with us in the end. Be careful.'

'Mama, who do all these things belong to?'

'I don't know,' answered Sofia. 'Now they're ours.'

'Mama, can we look in the wardrobe?'

'I'm going to the ghetto offices and I'll be right back,' said Sofia. 'Be quiet, because Aunt Stella is resting in the next room. And whatever you do, don't go down to the yard. Did you hear me?'

'Yes,' Yurik said.

Sofia went out and the boys were left by themselves.

'Should we open it?'

They opened the wardrobe door and slipped inside. 'There's nothing here,' said Yurik, disappointed. 'Just clothes.'

'I've found something,' Kazik exulted. 'It's a box to hide money in. I'll take it out.'

'Go down to the yard and get a brick, or a stone. I'll look for a screwdriver or something in the kitchen. Maybe we can open it.'

Kazik came back up from the yard with a brick. Yurik had found a screwdriver.

'Hold it, very firmly. Watch it, I'm going to give it a bang.'

'Boys, stop it,' shouted Stella from the next room.

'Just three more bangs,' Yurik promised.

'Let me,' pleaded Kazik.

'Move a second, I'm getting it.' Yurik had managed to pry the screwdriver under the top of the box and was hitting it now with the brick. The box suddenly buckled and opened. 'Damn it, I hurt my fingers!' He put his finger in his mouth and stamped his leg.

Kazik looked into the box. 'Foo, there's nothing but pictures.'

'Someone's coming,' said Yurik.

Kazik opened the door of their room a crack. 'It's just Mama,' he said.

Sofia entered Stella's room. 'Are you sleeping?'

Stella opened her eyes. 'No, just lying here.'

'Move a little.' Sofia pushed her over and sat down on the edge of the couch. 'I didn't accomplish anything.'

Stella had become Pan G.'s mistress. Pan G. was a German Jew who had come up in the world from his father's small shop to a position of authority, and he had excellent connections with the Gestapo. His pleasant face was always cleanly shaven. He would take care of Stella for as long as he wanted her and needed her money or Sofia's art collection, in order to have something to give to the Germans.

80

There was a knock on the door. It opened and Pani G. looked in shyly from behind the heavy lenses of her glasses. 'Can I offer you anything to drink?'

'No, thank you,' said Stella. 'We've just had something. Thanks very much, anyway.'

Pani G. stood for a moment in the doorway, smiling to no purpose and not knowing what to say. Finally she smiled even more broadly and shut the door.

'The poor woman,' said Sofia. 'Does he at least love his daughter?'

'Yes,' Stella said. 'The child he loves.'

'Have you spoken to him yet about Edek and your mother?'

'Yes. He promised to bring them here tomorrow afternoon. He seems to be hoping that by then there won't be anyone left to bring.'

The two of them were silent.

'The boys!' Sofia reminded herself. 'They haven't eaten lunch yet.' She got up and opened the pantry door. 'Boys,' she called.

'In a minute,' they answered.

'What should we do with the box?'

'Let's hide it,' Kazik suggested. 'On top of the wardrobe. Mama never cleans up there.'

'No, let's throw it out of the window,' Yurik said. It fell to the ground with a crash and they ran into the kitchen.

'Did you wash your hands?'

Yurik scanned the table. 'Sardines? Don't you know that I don't eat sardines?'

A strange man's voice came from the hall. Pani G. spoke to him for a minute and let him inside. He stood in the doorway, dressed in a large, cumbersome coat.

'This used to be my apartment,' he explained apologetically.

Sofia stood up embarrassedly. 'You can take whatever you want, of course,' she said quickly. 'Please, come on in.'

'You understand, my whole family . . .' He broke off in the middle. 'Silberstein,' he said, remembering to introduce himself. 'I'm going to try to get out of the ghetto. I left a few photographs in the wardrobe. That's really the only thing I came for,' he explained.

'Please go right ahead,' said Sofia.

He went to the boys' room.

'They're not there,' said Yurik before he got there. 'But I know where they are. Shall I bring them?'

'Yes, bring them,' said Sofia.

He called his brother and they both went down to the yard.

'I threw them right here under the window,' Yurik recalled. 'But I didn't think there were so many of them. Do you think someone else threw pictures here too?'

'Let's give him all of them. He'll know which are which.'

Yurik gathered up the photographs and the two boys went back up the stairs. There was an uncomfortable silence in the room. The man took the pictures, thanked them, and stuffed them into his large coat pockets. 'Goodbye,' he bowed.

They all said goodbye.

'Yurik, show Pan Silberstein to the door.'

'Why aren't you eating?' asked Sofia.

'I've already told you I don't like sardines.'

'That's all there is,' she said angrily. 'Eat them this minute.' Stella wanted to say something but restrained herself.

'I won't,' he said grandly and rose from the table.

'Sit down!'

He remained standing.

'Leave the room.'

Yurik whirled around and carelessly knocked the vase off the bookcase. There was a deathly silence in the room.

'That was our vase,' said Sofia. 'That was the last thing I still had from my mother's house.' She bent down and picked the pieces off the floor. 'Perhaps I can glue them,' she mused out loud. 'Get away from me, I don't need your help. I asked you to leave.'

Yurik left.

Yurik and Kazik dragged a broken-down sofa, its insides sticking out, through the yard.

'Here,' Yurik said.

They tipped it on its side against a wardrobe that was lying face-down on the ground. Yurik brought two chairs from the next courtyard. Kazik draped a striped mattress over the barricade.

'Go and get some more chairs.'

'Look, I've put a mattress on it, like in *Les Miserables*.'

'We have to leave a small hole to shoot through. We'll have a machine gun.'

'Hand grenades too.'

Yurik suddenly leaped on the sofa and shaded his eyes with his hand. 'They're coming!' he yelled.

Kazik lay down behind the sofa and began to fire.

'We forgot to put up a flag,' Yurik remembered. 'Go on shooting, I'll make one from this pillow. We'll have a red flag.'

He struggled with the hard fabric. 'I can't get it to tear,' he said angrily. He found a piece of broken glass and managed to cut a large square. He tied the flag to a stick and stood it on the barricade. 'At them!' he shouted.

'Ta-ta-ta-ta-ta!' went Kazik's machine gun. 'Bam! I threw a grenade.'

A breeze passing through the courtyard sucked up the feathers from the torn pillow and blew them this way and that.

Edek and Sofia's mother-in-law arrived the next day. The old lady's hair had grown even whiter after her husband's death, but she still carried her seventy years lightly on her unstooped shoulders. They didn't stay in the apartment for long, though. After a week of hiding in various parts of the house, from the attic to the basement, all of them were transferred by Pan G. to the workers' dormitory of the Karl Georg Schultz Military Apparel Industry. The adults went to work there, and life acquired a new routine. In the streets groups of Jews passed daily under armed guard on their way to the deportation square.

Sofia was already in bed.

'Get up, Soshka,' Edek awoke her. 'Go out on the balcony. The Russians are bombing.'

'Welcome to Warsaw!' one of the crowd gathered in the courtyard shouted up at the sky, waving his hands.

'Try to find a German in the streets now,' said Edek happily. 'Listen.'

From afar they heard the familiar scream of falling bombs and the rattle of anti-aircraft and machine-gun fire.

'Noch eine,' said the old woman in Yiddish, clapping her hands. 'A shayne bombeh.'

Sofia smiled. 'They're not falling only on Germans, Mama.'

'How unfair of them,' Edek mocked her.

She hugged her two boys to her. 'Fine, have it your way. Look, Kazhiula!' She turned the little boy's head.

The sky was spangled with colourful tracers, green, yellow and red. The long-armed beams of the searchlights crisscrossed back and forth, probing the velvety night.

Edek leaned out over the railing of the balcony. It was not the airplanes and bombs of the warring armies that he heard; it was the music of a new world, in which he believed with perfect faith, one that would bring a better future to human beings everywhere.

'Stella, get up, it's late already.' Sofia woke her.

Stella yawned and began to dress lazily. Sofia stood by the table and spread a piece of bread for Kazik. Her mother-in-law served coffee and began to make the beds, murmuring prayers under her breath. Edek sat on the bed, tying his shoes. He broke a shoelace.

'Shit!' he swore, throwing it on the floor.

The two boys smiled at the curse.

'Soshia, do you have a shoelace?'

'Look in the wardrobe where I put the old shoes. You'd better hurry if you still want to drink something.'

Edek drank his coffee standing up, buttoning his jacket with one hand.

'It's time you stopped walking around with that vial,' said Sofia, seeing him transfer the little bottle of poison from one pocket to another.

'Soshia, I've already told you, let me be.'

'One mustn't, one simply mustn't. One has to go on hoping till the last. It just isn't right.'

85

'I'm well aware of your theories by now,' he teased her.

'At least I don't argue with you about your politics,' she smiled. 'And I won't now. One day when the war is over we'll sit down and talk about who was right. You'd better hurry, Edek.'

Edek grabbed his hat and ran out. In the yard the men were already lined up by threes, waiting for the soldier who took them to work.

'Let me take Kazik with me today,' Stella suggested.

'Is that all right with you, Kazhiu?' Sofia asked him. 'I'll take you with me tomorrow,' she promised.

Sofia and Stella helped their mother up onto the high shelf in the corridor on which she hid, then they went down with the boys to the yard.

'Just look at my hands,' Sofia complained.

'You should put something on them. Or better still, get rubber gloves.'

'Mitek should just see two such hands!'

The two women parted. Stella took Kazik and went to the machine room. Sofia went up to the offices. She put on her apron and began to mop the floors. Yurik worked as a messenger boy for the book-keeping department.

The agreement signed between K. G. Schultz and the German authorities stipulated that the firm would employ eight hundred local Jewish workers whom the Germans would for the time being agree not to deport. In fact, at least two thousand people could easily have been counted in the factory and its dormitory.

That afternoon the police shut the gates of the factory. Their whistles and shouts filled the yard.

'Everybody downstairs!'

Groups of policemen quickly climbed to the top floors to seal off the roof and ferret out anyone hiding in the rooms.

Sofia took Yurik by the hand and went down with him to the yard.

'What's going to happen, Mama?'

'Nothing. Don't worry.'

'Listen. They're calling out names.'

Kosowsky, husband and wife! Rosenberg, husband and wife!

A couple standing near them moved forward in response. Sofia moved aside to let them through.

'They're going to tell us where to go now,' she tried to calm Yurik. 'Just keep standing quietly.'

The crowd of people kept moving towards the exit on the street. Soldiers and civilian police guarded the gate.

Sofia inched slowly forward, keeping a firm grip on Yurik's hand. A tight lump of fear constricted her throat. She stood on the tips of her toes to get a look at the soldiers sending each person off to live or to die. Who were they? What was their job back home? What had they studied at school? Did they love their girls? What power, religion, or lie had brought them to where they were now? Sofia squeezed her son's hand.

'What is it, Mama?'

'Nothing, Yurik. You're a good boy.'

'Pani Doctor, I think that to the right means deportation.'

Sofia turned around. Behind her was Doctor Wolff.

'Yes,' she said.

'*Rechts!*' the soldier yelled at her. Sofia pulled Yurik to the left. The soldier pushed her back the other way. '*Rechts!* Are you deaf or something?' The mild blue eyes of a child stared out from beneath his steel helmet.

'Mama,' said Yurik, 'he said to go to the right.'

'Yes, son. I heard him.'

87

They were made to sit in the street, near the pavement. Doctor Wolff sat down next to them.

'You too?' Sofia was amazed. 'I was sure you'd be sent to the left.'

Doctor Wolff nodded his head. 'What do they need a woman with a child for, or an old man with grey hair? Where's your brother the engineer?' he asked.

'Edek is working over on Ogrodowa Street. He was here late this morning, but the gates were already locked. He sent us a message that he's paid off one of the Jewish policemen for us. We'll just have to wait and see.'

'I have the feeling that we're in a bad position,' said the doctor. 'Those at the back always have a good chance of not fitting into the train and having to wait for the next one.'

'Let's try to move back while we're walking,' Sofia suggested.

Doctor Wolff scanned the still growing line. 'There must be close to seven hundred people,' he estimated.

Sofia searched for the policeman who had been bribed for them. She spotted him on the opposite pavement.

'Yurik, do you see him?'

'The one with the two bars?'

'Yes, with two bars on his hat. If he tells you to run and hide somewhere, I want you to listen to him. Don't look to see where I am. That's our policeman.'

Yurik nodded. 'Look, Mama,' he cried. 'I think that's Aunt Anna over there in the rickshaw.'

Sofia strained to see. 'Yes, that's Anna. Thank God, she's seen us.'

The rickshaw made a U-turn a few houses ahead of them and headed back the other way.

'Thank God!'

'Mama, I'm hungry,' Yurik whispered.

'I'll give you some sugar.' Sofia fumbled in her bag and gave him a handful of sugar cubes.

'Have some too, Doctor Wolff. I always keep a little sugar for an emergency.'

'No thank you,' he declined. 'Save it for the boy.'

'On your feet!'

They all rose.

'For-ward march!'

They marched in threes. Behind them they heard shots.

'Background music,' said Doctor Wolff.

'Halt! Sit down!'

They sat down again by the pavement.

'What are they shooting at?' asked Sofia.

'There's your answer,' said Doctor Wolff.

Several hearses emerged from a side street.

'It's all been prepared with exemplary German precision,' he said.

'On your feet! Forward march!'

They walked some more.

'Doctor Wolff,' Sofia reminded him, 'now's the time to start moving back.'

Their group was no different from any of the other deportations that were marched to the assembly point. A few armed soldiers guarded the head and the back of the line. A task force of Jewish police mounted on bicycles covered their left flank. A mixed detachment of soldiers and police covered the other flank.

'There's still hope,' said Doctor Wolff. 'Even if we don't manage to free ourselves on the way, there's a chance of getting away at the assembly point. And if we really are being shipped to labour camps, as they say, they'll probably need doctors there.'

'Where are you pushing, lady?'

'My daughter is back there,' Sofia apologized.

'Weren't you ever taught to walk on your own legs? Can't you see that we're all going forward?'

'Yes, I can see, Pani. But my daughter . . . Doctor Wolff, are you coming?'

'Yes, here I am.'

They had already worked their way back to the middle of the line. One of the soldiers noticed them.

'Where are you trying to go? Forward!'

'Yes,' Sofia repeated, 'forward.'

The soldier saw them slipping back again and lost his temper. He hit Sofia with his whip, and then Doctor Wolff. They managed to get to within three places of the end of the line. They were walking down the middle of the street now. Tree-shaded pavements extended on either side of them, behind which were empty houses. Here and there a curtain flapped in an open window, or laundry had been hung on a line.

The policeman with two bars edged close to Sofia and said without turning to look at her : 'Pani Doctor Kosow-olska? Tell the boy to go and hide in one of the houses. I'll look after you later. Tell him to hide and wait until I come for him.'

He walked away.

'Did you hear what he said, Yurik?'

'Mama, I'm not going anywhere without you.'

'You see that front gate? Run for it. Run!'

Yurik still clung to her. She pushed him from the line and he ran across the street and on through the open gate. Two Jewish policemen hurried after him and found him behind the staircase door. They dragged him back out to the street. A soldier came towards them waving a rubber club.

'You can let go,' said Yurik. 'I'll go back myself.'

The policemen released him. Yurik ran back, trying to

avoid the soldier. He almost succeeded. Only the tip of the club grazed his arm.

'You see, Mama, I told you.'

Sofia pressed him wordlessly to her. Theirs was the last deportation to reach the assembly point that day. The train wouldn't take them till tomorrow.

'Is this the *Unschlagplatz*?' asked Yurik.

'*Umschlagplatz*,' Sofia corrected him. 'It's German.'

Yurik had imagined it to be a muddy, blood-soaked field surrounded by high walls, each one higher than the next. In fact, they were standing by the last houses of the city, from which they were separated by a single red brick barrier. Not far in front of them passed the railway tracks, beyond which desolate fields stretched to the horizon. Barbed-wire fences, looped concertina-like between iron posts, were scattered here and there. The former vocational school building, now the Jewish hospital, rose before them. Sofia pulled Yurik towards it. The closer they got to it, the more crowded it became.

'We'll wait for it to get dark,' said Doctor Wolff.

'What time is it now?' she asked.

He looked at his watch. 'Five,' he said.

'Already? We started out at noon. I didn't notice the time go by. Yes, let's wait for it to get dark,' she agreed.

The sun was low in the sky.

'Look, Yurik.' Yurik glanced briefly at the sunset and went back to staring at the few lone trucks standing on the railway tracks. Sofia couldn't stop gazing at the splendour in the sky. She wiped her eyes with her hand. 'I'm sorry for getting so emotional,' she said to the doctor.

'Don't be sorry,' he smiled. 'Beauty is beauty here too.'

Sofia rolled down Yurik's sleeves. 'Button them,' she told him. 'It's going to start getting chilly now.'

The lights went on behind the barred windows of the hospital.

'If we can't get through the hospital,' said Doctor Wolff, 'I heard from someone that there was a wall around here which it's possible to climb over. We'll have to try to find it.'

'Pani Doctor Kosowolska and her son!'

'Doctor Alexander Wolff!'

'Nurse Steinberg!'

'Mama, we're being called.'

'Here we are! Here we are!' cried Sofia, pushing her way towards the hospital gates.

Anna's face peered through the peephole in the gate. 'Soshka, thank God!'

The gate opened slightly. There was a sudden crush as everyone near it tried to slip through. It shut again in their faces.

'Don't go away,' shouted Anna through the peephole.

The gate opened again and several burly orderlies, their arms linked together, barred the way. 'Pani Doctor? Follow us, please.'

They were catapulted through by the pressure of the crowd behind them. Doctor Wolff came too. The nurse couldn't be found. The orderlies struggled to shut the gate again. Dozens of hands clung to it from inside.

'Hands off! Hands off!'

The heavy gate swung shut with a dull clang. There was a terrible scream. Someone hadn't taken his hands off in time.

Sofia's and Yurik's bruises were attended to in the emergency room. One of the orderlies brought in the man whose fingers had been cut off. Anna took Yurik and Sofia out into the corridor.

'I'll hide Yurik here in the hospital,' she said. 'The day

after tomorrow there's an ambulance going out with convalescent children, and I hope we can get him back to the ghetto on it. Everything will be all right,' she said, turning to him. 'You'll lie here with the other children and pretend to be sick too. I'll come and visit you. Soshka, you take my papers and leave now with one of the nurses, who'll return them to me. How's Edek?'

'Edek is fine,' said Sofia distractedly, pulling Yurik towards her. 'You stay here,' she said. 'Will you promise to act like a grown-up person?'

Yurik nodded.

'Here are your papers and a little money, in case you need it. Guard the papers as though your life depended on it.'

'What about you?' he asked, alarmed.

'I'll go back to the factory. Come, give me a kiss.'

The boy stood on tiptoe to kiss his mother's cheek. Anna put her hand on Sofia's shoulder.

'Soshka, you must be out of here before the night shift comes on.'

Sofia straightened up. 'I'm ready. Go now, Yurik.'

The nurse who was waiting for him took him by the hand and led him down the corridor.

'Soshia!'

Edek, Stella and her old mother jumped up in surprise.

Edek looked at Sofia worriedly but was afraid to ask. The old woman couldn't restrain herself.

'Where's the boy?'

'Anna is hiding him in the hospital,' she reassured them. 'Everything is all right.'

The old woman calmed down. 'Kazik has eaten already and I've put him to bed,' she said. 'He behaved like a big boy. He's a fine little fellow.'

Sofia leaned over Kazik's bed. He was sleeping.

'How did you get here?' Edek asked.

Sofia slipped out of her shoes and began to tell them.

'Would you like something to eat?' Stella wanted to know.

'No. I can't eat. I'm just tired.' Her eyes shut and she lay down on the bed. 'Pan G. saw us at the factory gate and pretended he didn't,' she said.

Stella didn't answer. Her mother lay down too.

Edek and Stella sat up whispering at the table for a long time. It was late at night when they turned out the light. Sofia still hadn't fallen asleep.

'Come, Kazhiula, let's go upstairs.' She picked up the bucket and Kazik followed her, dragging the mop.

'What was it like with Aunt Stella yesterday? Did you miss me?'

'It was fine,' he said.

'Give me the mop, I have to finish off. It's getting awfully late.' She took the wet rag from the bucket and handed him one end.

'Hold it tight and I'll wring it out. But really tight.'

Policemen shouted and blew their whistles in the yard. Sofia threw down the rag and grabbed Kazik's hand. 'Come quick.'

This time, she decided, she wasn't going down, come what may. She and Kazik stepped out into the hallway next to the infirmary. The infirmary door opened and two doctors emerged.

'Are you going down, Pani Doctor?'

'No, I'm staying here.'

The doctors started down and she shut the staircase door

94

behind them. She opened the top of the linen bin.

'Come on, Kazhiula, get in here. If I'm not back by the time it gets dark, get out and go to Aunt Stella's. But only when it gets dark. Will you remember?' She helped him into the bin. 'Don't forget what I told you.'

The boy nodded. Sofia kissed him hurriedly on the head and shut the top of the bin.

'Are you comfortable in there?'

'Yes,' he said.

'God bless you. Don't forget to stay in there.'

She hurried to the staircase door. The moment she opened it she realized that she was trapped. The police were already combing the upper floors. Her mind was a blank. She started down the stairs, leaving the door wide open behind her. The stairs led her down to the basement. She passed through several narrow, damp corridors, groping her way slowly along in the darkness. The corridor suddenly swung to the left and ended. Her hands ran into a wall. She turned and leaned against it. It surprised her that she felt no distress. She tried to make out what she did feel, but there was only a curious nothingness.

'Mama! Mama!'

She didn't budge. Was that Kazik calling? Her foot encountered a sack. She pulled it over to her and sat down on it. The police were on the ground floor. She could hear them running through the rooms. They were dragging someone out. She heard their hurried footsteps on the stairs. Somebody was trying to escape. Just let him not come in here, she pleaded. God Almighty! Let them catch him before he got to her. She heard him running down the wooden stairs that led to the basement. He tripped on something and fell. The policemen pounced on him and dragged him out to the courtyard.

The noise died down. She heard the gates being locked.

Two men crossed the yard and descended the stairs. They entered the basement and shone a flashlight into it.

'Enough, no one's here,' said one of them.

Sofia spread out the sack and lay down on it. She had to wait. What time was it? She tried to make out the dial of her watch but she couldn't see a thing. She mustn't come out yet. She put her fingers on her wrist and began taking her pulse to count the minutes. The silence rang in her ears. An intolerably oppressive sense of helplessness was invading the vacuum inside her.

And all her life she had prided herself on her ability to lead a rational existence! She lay there in the dark corner of the basement with nothing to do.

Kazik decided to leave the linen bin. He wasn't comfortable inside. He opened the top and got out. He went to the window. He tried to find his mother among the people in the courtyard but couldn't make her out. Hasty footsteps on the stairs gave him a fright and he jumped back into the bin. Through the cracks in the wood he saw two pairs of legs step into the corridor and walk down it. One of them stopped by the bin.

'Frank, come here. There's a big chest here.'

'I'm coming,' said the other.

Kazik could feel them trying to lift him.

'It's not heavy,' he heard a voice say above him. 'We could throw it down on the Jew bastards in the yard.'

'Come here,' said the second voice. 'There's another door to the same room.'

Kazik heard the two of them going through more and more distant rooms and then coming back down the corridor. One of them sat on the linen bin.

'Open the window and throw down a chair.'

'You can let them have that stool there into the bargain.'
They burst out laughing and went down the stairs.

'Mama, I have to go,' Kazik whispered to himself. He was afraid to leave the linen bin. For a while he managed to hold it in. 'Mama,' he whispered again. In the end he decided to pee through one of the cracks. Would he get into trouble for it? His mother would clean it up. That made him feel better. He peeped out. It can't get far, he thought, watching the puddle spread over the floorboards. He put his head down on the dirty linen, hugged his knees with his hands, and fell fast asleep.

Sofia opened the linen bin and looked at him for a long time. 'Kazhiula!' She picked him up and rested his curly head on her shoulder. He opened his eyes.

'Are you back already, Mama?' He shut them again.

'Just a second,' she said. 'I don't have the strength to carry you like this in my arms. Let me take you piggy-back.'

Without opening his eyes he let her stand him on a chair.

'You're choking me,' she said, loosening his grip a little. He wrapped his arms around her neck.

The door to their room was wide open. Sofia walked in and switched on the light. 'Mother!' she called.

'Soshia? Thank God you're here. I thought you'd never come back. They were here, but they didn't see me.'

'I'll help you down in a second,' said Sofia. 'Let me just get Kazik to bed. The poor little fellow fell asleep.'

Stella came in and shut the door behind her. 'Soshia?'

'Yes, I'm back.'

Stella helped her mother off the shelf.

'Edek hasn't come yet?' she asked.

'No. Have you seen G.?'

97

'I saw him,' Stella said. 'By chance he was where Edek works on Ogrodowa Street during the selection there. He says he didn't see Edek.'

Their eyes met. Stella turned to the window.

'Which means . . .' Sofia began, and then trailed off. She took a box of matches and went to the stove. The matches wouldn't light. One after another they broke in her hand.

'Don't bother,' the old woman shooed her away, 'I'll make supper.'

Sofia handed her the matches and went to Kazik's bed. 'Get up, Kazhiula.' She shook him gently. 'We still haven't washed ourselves today.'

The nurse brought Yurik to the children's ward. She stopped by one of the beds. 'You lie here, next to this girl,' she said. 'But be careful not to push her. She's very sick.'

'Side by side, or upside down like playing cards?' he asked.

The nurse laughed. 'Like cards,' she said. She rolled back the blanket by the girl's legs. 'Well, what are you waiting for?'

'In my clothes?'

'All right, you can take them off and lie in your underwear. But put your clothes under your pillow and keep your eye on them. Supper will be served soon,' she announced loudly and left the room.

Yurik remained sitting on the bed. There were so many children, he thought.

'What's the matter with you?' he asked the girl.

'A bullet went right through me and came out at the back,' she whispered. 'It made a hole.'

'Will they shave my head like yours?'

'Only if you're here a long time,' she replied.

Yurik turned to look at the faces watching him from the nearby beds.

'You can't tell the boys from the girls,' he said. That must be a girl, he thought, looking at a pair of blue eyes staring from a shaven head.

The girl slipped out of her bed and crawled on her knees to his.

'What's your name?'

'Jerzy Henryk Kosowolski, but I'm called Yurik.'

'My name's Sara,' she said.

A Jewish name, Yurik thought. 'Would you like a sweet?' He took a handful of boiled sweets from his pocket and offered them to her. She took one and thanked him.

He treated the other children near him too. He's got sweets, he heard them whisper. He felt in his pocket for more but couldn't find any.

'Just a minute,' he said. 'Maybe in my other pocket.'

He put his hand into his other pocket and pulled out a handkerchief, which he put on the blanket. He took out some bottle-tops, four lead soldiers, a piece of string, a French coin, a box of postage stamps, a metal tap from his shoe, a penknife, the tooth of a fork, and a few playing cards. Then he turned the pocket inside out. 'I don't have any more,' he said, disappointed.

He sat down on the bed and began unlacing his shoes. Sara reached out to touch his clothes.

'What nice clothes,' she exclaimed. 'Who gave them to you?'

'My mother,' he said.

'You have a mother? Where is she?'

'In a factory. I have a father too. He's an officer in our army and a doctor. He's in Russia now.'

A boy said something to him in Yiddish.

'I don't understand that language,' he said proudly. 'What

99

happened to your feet?' he asked Sara.

She told him about some Polish boys who caught her smuggling bread and threw her into a pit full of snow.

'I lay in it all night long,' she said. She pointed to her feet : 'They froze and came off.'

Yurik finished undressing and put his clothing under the mattress.

'Did the nurse tell you to do that?'

'Yes,' he said.

'She thinks we're all thieves,' Sara said.

The door opened and two nurses came into the room, pushing a trolley bearing food for supper. The children scattered back to their beds.

'How old are you?' he asked Sara the next day.

'Sixteen,' she said. 'If I had my hair you'd see I was big.'

'What kind of hair did you have?'

'Blonde. Not all of it, though. Do you want to see some?'

'Yes,' he said.

She took out a bundle of rags from beneath her mattress and opened it. 'Here,' she showed him a curl of blonde hair. 'I had long braids, but after the typhus it grew back curly.'

'Did you hear them shooting last night?'

'Yes. They shoot outside every night.'

'They don't come in here?'

'Just the German doctors in uniform,' Sara said. 'They go from bed to bed and go away. You'll see them today. Do you hear all that crying?'

'Yes,' he said.

'They're loading people onto the trains. You can see it

from the bathroom window if you'd like. Come on, I'll go with you.' She got out of bed and accompanied him on all fours.

'Right here. Pull up a chair and climb on it. I'll wait down here. I've already seen it lots of times.'

Yurik climbed on the chair and looked out.

'Let's go back,' he said to her after a while. 'I've seen enough.'

He helped her back to the big room.

'With support I can walk standing up,' she boasted.

'Doesn't it hurt?'

'Just a little bit. It's not so bad. After the war they'll buy me a pair of those special shoes and I'll be able to get around all by myself.'

The next morning the convalescent children were sent home from the hospital. Yurik got dressed and put on his shoes. He was already on his way out of the room when he heard someone calling his name. Sara came up to him, holding the folder with his papers in her mouth. 'You forgot this.'

He took the folder and stuck it in his pocket.

'Is your mother pretty?' she asked.

'Yes,' he said.

They were silent. Yurik put his hand in his pocket to look for a present to give her but couldn't find anything. He felt suddenly embarrassed.

'Hey there, hurry up, we're going!' Yurik spun around and left. He was wearing shorts and a polo shirt, and his socks flopped over his shoes. Don't read your emotions into him. He wasn't at all upset. He was sure that this was how it was supposed to be.

6

Stella was born after Mitek, who was the eldest. The third child was Mania, an ordinary girl who married as soon as she could and opened a bakery with her husband in the Jewish quarter of Warsaw. Mundek was the next. The prodigal son. Mundek joined the Communist Party when he was still a young man. He was tall and terribly athletic; once, while trying to elude the police in Paris, he had jumped off a bridge over the Seine. He returned in one piece from the Spanish Civil War, and occasionally sent his parents in Warsaw a photograph of himself in a long coat and a hat, on the back of which it said :

There's nothing underneath. Just my bones.

Your son,

Mundek.

Whenever such a photograph arrived, the old man would go off to the post office and mail his son a cheque. 'He'll give it all to that damned party of his anyway,' he would sigh as he signed it. He himself made an occasional donation to the Jewish National Fund and had even spent a few months in Palestine. He had dreamed that his oldest son would study agronomy and settle in the Holy Land, but Mitek had had other ideas.

Ella was the last-born. As a child she had always been pale, thin and oversensitive, ready to burst into tears at the slightest pretext. Sometimes she would grab her face with her bony hands and scream in distress :

'My eyes! Ouch, my eyes!'

Her parents took her from doctor to doctor, going as far as Vienna, but no cure for her was found. She's hypochondriac, said the doctors, neurasthenic, perhaps even brain-damaged. Finally they took her to Doctor Zamenhof, the inventor of Esperanto, who lived a few blocks away. He turned up an eyelid and extracted some long lashes with thin little tweezers.

'You've got the most lovely eyelashes,' he smiled at the girl.

'Is it true that you've invented a new language, Pan Doctor?' she plucked up the courage to ask.

'It most certainly is,' he nodded puckishly. 'And it will unite all nations, and all people, too.'

That was the end of Ella's eye trouble. Ella liked to read poetry out loud. She liked soldiers and churchbells. She fell in love with an air force officer and, after becoming a Catholic, married him. For years she never visited her parents, who consented to see her again only after her husband was shot down over Warsaw at the outbreak of the war. She and the pilot's mother, a wizened, pious old Catholic bereaved of her only son, were inseparable. Ella was still the same pale-faced, nervous girl she had always been, sensitive to beauty and apt to fall in love. Piles of novels and poetry books lay scattered on her night-table by an overflowing ashtray. Sofia called her affection-ately 'the brave coward'. She was the aunt for reading stories, too.

Ella received a message from her friend G. to appear one morning at the Schultz factory's branch on the Polish side of Warsaw to pick up Yurik, Kazik and Yoasha, and bring them to the safety of the Polish houses where it had been arranged they would be hidden. The sudden rush to trans-fer them was the result of a new regulation forbidding the children of workers to stay with their parents in the factory. Anna decided to send Yoasha with Sofia's two boys, and one morning the three of them passed through the ghetto gates with those of Schultz's employees who worked on the Polish side.

'I've already been in the *Umschlagplatz* once, and Kazik was almost thrown through the window in a chest.'

Yoasha had nothing of her own to brag about.

A doorman was energetically sweeping the pavement. A man in civilian dress, with a hat and an official's leather briefcase, passed in front of him.

'Good morning, sir,' said the doorman.

The official halted. 'How's work, Valenti?'

The doorman paused and leaned against his broom. 'Ah, there's plenty of it, sir. The pavements keep getting dirty.'

Yoasha emerged from the house holding Ella by the arm. The two of them strolled along chatting. Valenti gazed after them and remarked : That Pani Kosowolska, if you don't mind my saying so, sir. Just the other day she gave me some change to help me carry some suitcases for her. She must be doing business with the Jews. It's not a bad business either, I can tell you. They'll give anything for something to eat. Bring them a sausage, a herring, some eggs, and they'll fit you out with clothing from head to foot, with enough left over for your wife. If you'd be so kind as to move a little, sir, you'd be out of the way of the dust. I've never seen such bad times. They're grabbing real Poles off the streets nowadays and sending them God only knows where. Some say to work in Berlin, and others' – he lowered his voice – 'to Auschwitz, to the concentration camp. You don't know when you leave for work in the morning if you'll ever come home at night.'

Yurik and Kazik came out of the house into the street. Valenti measured them with a glance. 'Jews,' he remarked, dismissing them with a wave of his hand. 'It's a shame about the little ones, if you know what I mean, sir, but what can anyone do? In the end they're bound to be caught. Two boys like that, wearing raincoats and carrying a briefcase, won't get far. Not with all the young punks roaming the streets these days and sniffing after Jews, they won't! They'll stick 'em up for what money they have, and if they haven't got any – it's off to the police with them for the reward. To think of what we've come to.' Valenti let out a sigh. 'I myself wouldn't mind hiding a little Jew or two at my place, it's not a free service, after all. But my old lady's as scared as a rabbit. She hasn't got the nerves for it. . . . Well, I'll be seeing you, sir,' he said, touching a finger to the brim of his cap. 'If you should happen to have a little suitcase yourself, or anything else you'd like me to do for you. . . .'

'I'll keep you in mind, Valenti,' promised the official. He walked down the street and was gone.

Yurik and Kazik strolled along the street.

'She said to turn left at the first corner,' said Yurik.

'Yes,' Kazik said.

'And then to keep going straight till we get to number twenty-two.'

They reached the corner and turned left, straining to catch sight of a house number. 'It's still a long way,' Yurik said. 'Let's walk faster.'

They reached number twenty-two and entered the yard.

'Are you sure this is it?' Kazik asked.

'That's what Aunt Ella said,' answered Yurik.

They stood against the wall by the door to the stairway, underneath the letter boxes.

'When will she come?'

Yurik shrugged.

'Someone's coming down the stairs,' whispered Kazik.

'Quick, let's pretend that we're talking.'

'Yurik and Kazik?' The man on the stairs called out their names.

'Yes, here we are.'

'Who's Yurik and who's Kazik?'

'I'm Yurik,' said the older brother, 'and he's Kazik.'

The man ran his hand through the smaller boy's curls. 'Don't be worried,' he said. 'The lady who's coming for you will be here soon. All you have to do is keep standing right here. I take it I can leave you here by yourselves. You're a big boy, keep an eye out.'

'I will,' Yurik said.

'Goodbye, boys.'

'Goodbye.'

'He's gone,' Kazik said. 'Do you know why they call our factory Karl Georg Schultz?'

'That's Schultz's name.'

'That's not what I mean,' said Kazik. 'I mean why it has got three names. Listen. Once there was a man named Karl, and another man named Georg, and another man named Schultz.'

'Are you making it up?' Yurik asked.

'Yes. One day . . .' Two men in civilian clothes entered the stairway and stopped when they saw the two boys.

'One day the three of them went for a walk in a field and Karl kept pulling up grass.'

One of the men, who was the taller of the two and wore a grey suit, said something to Yurik. The man in the brown suit just looked at them.

'I don't understand German,' Yurik answered.

'*Jude?*' asked Grey Suit.

Yurik shrugged. 'No,' he said.

They took the two boys into the yard, stood them against the front gate, and began to interrogate them. Yurik answered their questions, trying as hard as he could to outfox them, at times helplessly saying nothing, at others anything at all.

'Where do you live?'

'I don't know. Nowhere.'

'*Jude?*'

'No.'

Grey Suit slapped him in the face. 'Who brought you here?'

'A lady,' said Yurik.

'Where is she?'

'She's coming soon.'

'Are you a Jew?'

'No.'

Grey Suit slapped Yurik again. The two men exchanged whispers and decided to wait for the lady to come.

'What's her name?'

Yurik shrugged. The two of them grabbed him and shook him hard. 'What's her name?' Grey Suit shouted in his face.

'I'm telling you, I don't know,' Yurik said, frightened.

'What's your name?'

'Jerzy Henryk.'

'Henryk, Henryk,' the man repeated the name. 'Jude Henryk maybe, eh?'

The boy denied it again in a whisper, turning his face. The blow glanced off his arm and knocked the beret from his head. Kazik bent down to pick it up.

'Take the briefcase too,' Yurik said. Before the two men could react he was running up the stairs, taking them several at a time. They both drew their guns and rushed after him.

Kazik remained in the yard. He stood there for a moment uncertainly, then picked up the briefcase and followed them. The stairs were steep and he climbed them slowly.

Yurik pushed open the first door he came to and shouted

at the frightened people inside : 'Tell Pani Kosowolska . . .'
The two men grabbed him. One held his arms while the
other beat him viciously.

When he came to he was lying on the floor. He opened
his eyes to see his brother staring at him from the doorway.
He slowly turned his head and saw a small crowd of men
and women at the end of the corridor looking at him in
frightened silence. The two men who had grabbed him
stood over him. He heard one of them ask :

'Does anyone here know a woman named Henryk?
Henryk? Where's the house list?'

Yurik mechanically put his hand in his jacket pocket and
laid a hundred crown note at their feet. Grey Suit pushed
it away with his shoe. Yurik picked it up and put it back in
his pocket. They grabbed him by the arms and dragged
him back out to the yard.

Ella came out of an office on the courtyard and saw the
two boys standing by the front gate with two strange men.
She glanced at them indifferently as she passed through the
yard and went out through the gate to the street. Neither
of the boys tried to signal her.

'It looks like she's not coming,' said one of the two
men after a long while. 'We might as well go.'

Yurik put up a fight. He squirmed, kicked and scratched
their hands. They twisted his arm behind him and
marched him out to the street. He began to pray out loud.

'In the name of the Father, the Son, and the Holy
Ghost. Our Father Who art in heaven, hallowed be Thy
name, Thy kingdom come, They will be done. . . .'

They paid him no attention.

'. . . forgive us our trespasses as we forgive those who
trespass against us,' he continued to pray, sobbing and
crossing himself over and over. Kazik dragged a few steps
behind, carrying the briefcase and his brother's beret.

'See,' said a mother passing by on the street to her small girl. 'He hit his little brother and now he's getting what he deserves. The same will happen to you if you're bad.'

Yurik's sobs subsided into irregular gasps. He suddenly remembered his papers from the factory. He took them out and handed them to the men. They looked at them and began to laugh.

'*Bist du Jude?*' asked one of them.

Yurik didn't answer. The two men took them to a blind, deserted side street that was flanked by the ghetto wall. They stood the boys against the bricks and backed off a few paces. They drew their pistols and cocked them with a click. Yurik nudged his brother with an elbow.

'Kazik, they're going to kill us.'

Kazik nodded comprehendingly. 'Take your beret,' he said.

A German officer, who happened to notice them from his carriage, told the two men to take the boys to the *Umschlagplatz* for legal processing. The two gave him a Hitler salute and brought the boys to the nearest police station.

'Jewish?' asked the sergeant on duty.

'No,' Yurik said.

'Get undressed.'

Yurik took off his jacket and began pulling off his shirts, first one, then another, then a third. The policemen burst out laughing. 'That's enough,' said the sergeant. 'You can get dressed.'

He led the two boys to the waiting-room and pointed at the bench reserved for Jews. 'Sit here.'

'Yurik,' whispered Kazik. 'Look at those two in the corner. They must be thieves.'

'Right,' said Yurik, lying down on the bench. He was dizzy and his whole body ached.

'Yurik,' Kazik prodded him, 'look at that fat woman.'

Yurik opened his eyes. A buxom lady sat across from them, eating breakfast with the sergeant on duty. Every now and then the two burst into loud laughter.

Yurik shut his eyes again and dozed off. He awoke when a girl his age sat down next to him on the bench and started to cry.

'Where did they get you?'

'They caught me with a loaf of bread,' she said. 'The officer asked me if I knew I could get the death penalty for smuggling food. Of course I know.' She began to cry again.

Yurik sat up and opened the briefcase. He took out their sandwiches and offered her one. 'Would you like some?'

'Yes.'

He gave a piece to Kazik and bit into what was left. It made him nauseous.

'Take mine too,' he said to her, and lay down again. His mother was coming towards him quickly. She was wearing her black fur coat. It grew larger as it approached him like a rolling ball, wrapping him in its warmth.

'Yurik,' Kazik nudged him, 'wake up for a minute.'

'What do you want?'

'I have to go.'

Yurik raised himself up on one elbow. 'Where's the girl?'

'The policeman took her away.'

'What are you embarrassed for?' he said angrily, seeing Kazik hop from foot to foot. 'Go and tell the policeman over there. Go on!"

Kazik walked to the bench opposite them. 'Please, officer . . .'

The sergeant was leaning over his lady friend's bosom, whispering something in her ear.

'Officer?'

She noticed him first. 'What is it, you little darling?'
'I have to go to the bathroom.'
'Get up and go with him.' She slapped the sergeant's behind.
The two thieves in the corner roared with laughter.
'Quiet there, you sons of bitches!' He shook his fist at them. The laughter stopped.
'Come on, sonny boy,' he said with fond self-esteem. 'I'll take you.'
Yurik dozed off.
'Yurik, there are soldiers drilling in the yard. You should go and look.'
Silence.
'Yurik?'
'Leave me alone.'
'Yurik?'
'What the hell do you want?'
'I'm going again. You come too.'
Yurik sat up on the bench. 'What time is it?' he asked.
'It's noon already.'

A police corporal waited for them to return. He led the two boys out into the street. It was a fine warm day. The afternoon sun overhead all but washed away the shadows of the houses. The pavements dazzled their eyes.
'Look what a moustache he has,' said Kazik behind the corporal's back.
The policeman noticed them admiring it. 'You'll have one too one day. It just takes a little patience. Would you like something to drink?'
'I would,' said Yurik.
The corporal stopped at a kiosk and bought each boy a cold lemonade.

'Where did you get two such big boys from?' asked the vendor, handing him his change.

'They're not mine,' he said.

'You never know,' she laughed.

He wagged his finger at her. 'I'll have you arrested, you brazen woman,' he joked.

Two rickshaws, each with an SS officer in full regalia, stood under the wooden bridge by the ghetto gate. About a dozen Jewish and Polish policemen were clustered around them. Sofia, who had been called urgently from the factory, stood between the rickshaws, a short, frightened woman dressed in a grey work smock.

'What's going on?' asked one of the policemen stationed at the gate.

'Some officer caught her kids on the Polish side. Here they come.'

The corporal appeared, holding the two boys by the hand. The sentry at the gate pointed his rifle at them.

Yurik took fright. 'He's going to kill us,' he said. 'Please take us through the gate,' he asked the corporal.

The corporal saw them through, saluted, and went off.

'Here's Mama,' said Kazik, spying her.

A Jewish policeman went through their pockets. He didn't find the hundred crown note but he did find the handsome Finnish penknife that Yoasha had given Yurik for his birthday. 'I'll take this for my son,' he said.

But the penknife passed on to a Polish policeman, then to a sergeant, and then to the SS officer sitting in the left-hand rickshaw, on whose seat it remained.

'I'll send it to Hans back in Hanover,' he told his colleague. 'Bring me the woman,' he ordered.

Sofia was brought to him.

'Your papers!'

She took out her papers with trembling hands and gave them to him. He took them and tore them to pieces with a laugh. 'Who are you now?' he shouted right in her face.

She retreated a step, instinctively clutching her children. 'Well, why don't you take them away?' he said to the soldiers.

The two rickshaws turned around and passed back through the gate. The soldiers and the policemen saluted as they left. The Jewish policemen took Sofia and the two boys to a police station. Sofia took advantage of several minutes in which they were left to themselves to enter the kitchen in the back. A woman in an apron was stirring a pot on a stove. Sofia offered her her watch. 'Please,' she implored. 'I have two boys. You don't have to go far, just to the Schultz factory, and give this note to Pan G. I beg you.'

The woman hesitated but finally agreed. She took the watch, put on her coat and left. Sofia returned to the waiting-room and sat down next to Yurik, who was dozing.

'Pani Kosowolska, to the head office please!'

Sofia followed the desk sergeant with her two boys. Three high-ranking police officials sat behind a green-covered table.

'Pan Advocate,' said Sofia in surprise to the one on the left.

The official rose and looked at her.

'Pani Doctor Kosowolska!' He shook her hand. 'Are these your boys? How they've grown.'

'Prepare two rickshaws!' he ordered. The sergeant left the office.

'I have no choice but to send you to the *Umschlag-platz*,' he said to Sofia. 'The authorities are likely to check all the names on their list. There are no trains going out today, so I'll be able to arrange to have you escorted back again. The same policeman will bring you back today to the factory. The best of luck to you.' He kissed her hand.

'I don't know how to thank you. I . . .' There were tears in her eyes.

'Don't mention it,' he smiled. 'Goodbye now,' He reached out over the table and rumpled Kazik's curls.

Two policemen took them to the *Umschlagplatz* in two rickshaws. Yurik dozed all the way. He awoke to find the policemen carrying him up the stairs of the hospital. They were brought to a special detention room where an attending policeman wrote down their names. In the room were a teenage boy and girl, and an old woman who sat groaning on the window sill. The boy had just finished carving his name in the plaster on the wall; he wiped his hands on the back of his trousers and lay down on the bench next to the girl, resting his head on her knees so that his cap slipped down over his face. Sofia sat opposite them. 'Is he your brother?' she asked the girl. 'You look awfully alike. What's the difference in age between you?'

'Two years. I'm seventeen.'

'You came here of your own free will?'

'Yes,' said the girl. 'We're the only ones left in our family. There's nothing to eat, and we can't go on hiding any more. They gave us bread and jam as soon as we got here. That's how it is when you volunteer.'

'Yurik, should we write our names?'

'Do you have something to do it with?'

'I've got a nail.'

'You go and write them. I don't feel like it. The date too, don't forget,' he reminded him. Kazik went to the wall.

The policemen came to take them back. The rickshaws were still waiting for them outside. The sentries paid no attention to them as they passed. Once the *Umschlagplatz* was gone from sight, the two rickshaw drivers got down off their bicycles. 'Pani, we haven't been paid for the way back yet.'

One of the policemen lost his temper. 'Goddamn it!' he cried. 'I told you we were making a round trip.'

'No, you didn't,' they protested. 'And we had to wait for you an hour and a half at the *Umschlagplatz*.'

They argued and finally agreed on half-fare. The policeman sat down again next to Sofia. The rickshaw drivers remounted their bicyles and pedalled on. Sofia looked at her children. Kazik sat gaping at the buildings on the deserted streets. Yurik had fallen asleep again with his head against the policeman.

7

Yurik opened the door of the office and snapped to attention. There went Schultz! A row of men passed by him into the room. Yurik shut the door after them and remained standing there in order to open it again at the right moment. No, they weren't done yet. It was just somebody moving his chair.

Sofia came up the stairs. 'Yurik.'

'Yes.'

'Listen, Yurik.' Sofia paused. 'I want you to ask Pan Witkowski to arrange for new papers for me,' she said, for some reason embarrased in front of the child. 'Maybe he'll agree if he's asked by a boy. Do you know which one he is?'

'Yes. The tall Polish one.'

'That's right. Now listen carefully. You're to tell him that your father, Doctor Kosowolski, an officer in the Polish army, is a prisoner in Russia, and that your mother is here without any papers because a German officer tore them up the other day. Tell him that your mother would be very grateful if he could arrange new papers for her, and that your father will thank him after the war. Did you get that? Tell him that it's a matter of life and death for us.'

Yurik understood. Sofia wanted to add something but stopped herself. 'I'll wait for you in the yard down below,' she said.

Yurik opened the door. Schultz, a stocky giant of a man, was the first to leave the room. Pan Witkowski was among the last.

'Excuse me,' Yurik began.

Pan Witkowski halted and inclined his tall body a fraction. 'What can I do for you, young man?'

'My mother asked,' said Yurik. 'My father is an officer in the Polish army, he's in Russia now. Doctor Kosowolski. Could you perhaps get my mother new papers? My father will thank you very much after the war. It's a matter of life and death for us.'

Pan Witkowski straightened up. 'I'm very sorry, young man, but it's simply not in my jurisdiction.' He walked away with long steps.

Yurik felt the ground slipping away from under him. He had called in vain upon that which was most sacred to him : his father the officer, the doctor, who had told them so many war stories and sketched the battles for them in their sandbox with his finger. He went down to the yard. His mother was waiting for him there.

'Mama,' he said, clutching her. He began to sob silently, for a long time.

'He said it wasn't in his jurisdiction.'

Stella said nothing.

'Yurik cried,' Sofia said.

The old woman spat in anger. 'May that damned Pole rot in hell!'

'What will become of us?' Sofia mused, glancing at the two children sleeping in their beds.

Stella rose and went to the mirror, where she started to make up her face. Sofia followed her silently with her eyes, and said : 'Take Edek's gold cigarette case. And the miniature.'

'Should I wear my white earrings?'

'Yes,' said Sofia. 'They're very becoming on you.'

Sofia took out the things and put them on the table. Stella opened the wardrobe door and looked at herself in the full-length mirror.

'Good night, Soshka. Perhaps I can make use of the opportunity to get you a nice new apartment in the bargain. Don't wait up for me, Mama, do you hear? I'll be back late.'

The old woman buried her face in her hands and lapsed into prayer by the darkened window where she stood.

'Now we'll live all by ourselves,' Sofia said, showing the children around the apartment. 'You'll sleep here, Yurik, and I'll sleep with Kazik in the other room.'

'But this is a baby's bed,' Yurik protested. 'Look, it's just like a cot.'

'It's all right, it's big enough. You can try it out straightaway.'

Yurik lay down on the bed and straightened his legs.

'There, you see? It's just the right size.'

Sofia lit a candle and put it on the floor beneath the table. 'Tomorrow we'll black out the windows,' she promised. 'In honour of our new apartment we're going to have a royal banquet and I won't even make you wash first.'

She opened the pantry and took out some plates stacked high with sandwiches that had been prepared in advance. 'Would you look at that!' she marvelled. 'We'll sit on the floor and have a picnic.' She poured tea for them all.

'Kazhiula, if you want some more sugar you can take as much as you like tonight.'

'Even a whole spoonful?'

'But you'll throw up from all that sweetness! Oh well, take two then. I think I'll have a wash after all,' she decided. She poured some water into the sink and began to undress.

The two boys went to the other room and sat on the bed. 'Wait for me there,' she told them. 'And don't fight. I'll come and tell you stories when I'm ready.'

'How does the Karl Georg Schultz story end?' Yurik asked Kazik.

'I don't know,' Kazik said. 'I've forgotten.'

'Brrrr, it's cold,' said Sofia, coming in wrapped in a robe. 'But there's nothing like soap and water. It makes one feel born anew.'

She sat between them.

'About when you were little,' Yurik requested.

'Yes, when you were little,' Kazik repeated.

'About when I was little?' she smiled. 'I was very little and I had long braids.'

'But they were brown,' Yurik said.

'Brown, that's right. Don't you like brown hair?'

'I'd rather it was blonde.'

'Should I dye it like Aunt Ella's?'

'No, she's a redhead.'

Sofia lapsed into thought, swaying rhythmically back and forth with the children.

'Well?' Yurik roused her. 'Why don't you tell us something.'

'Yes,' she remembered. 'What should I tell you about? I've already told you about the pudding.'

'Yes, how you kicked it.'

'And about the fat priest and the umbrella?'

'Right in the stomach,' said Yurik.

'And about the time we went rowing and would have drowned if not for Uncle Edek?'

'You've told us that too,' said Kazik.

'And about . . .' She tried to think. 'About the wonderful old teacher I once had?'

'That's not interesting,' said Yurik. 'Tell us, you know, something with an adventure.'

'Once I took a train ride with your father,' she began. 'It was our first trip to Paris. Papa went there to study medicine. We had learned French at home, but we were afraid to talk it to the Frenchmen in case they wouldn't understand.'

'I know,' said Yurik. 'There was a lady in your compartment, and you argued all the way to Paris about who should talk to her, and when you got there she asked you in Polish where some street was. I know that story. I don't call that an adventure.'

'What can I do? I've never had any adventures. Oh, yes, once somebody tried to steal my suitcase in the station.'

'By throwing ink on your coat to distract you,' Yurik remembered.

'You see, you know that one too.'

'All right, tell us something else. Tell us a book.'

'Robin Hood,' said one of the boys.

'Robin Hood!' they both enthused.

'But you've read the book yourselves!'

'It doesn't matter, tell it to us.'

In no time the room had turned into Sherwood Forest and the two boys listened open-mouthed to the story of brave Robin Hood, dressed all in green, who robbed the rich and gave to the poor.

'I'll be a Robin Hood when I'm big,' said Kazik.

The next day a new and unexplained regulation was issued :

ALL RESIDENTS WITHOUT EXCEPTION MUST REPORT TODAY TO THE MILA STREET STATION. BRING ENOUGH FOOD FOR THREE DAYS. LEAVE ALL APARTMENTS OPEN. ALL NOT COMPLYING WILL BE SHOT.

'What do they have in store for us this time?'

'The devil knows,' grumbled Stella.

The old woman got out of bed and pulled on her woollen stockings. Sofia spoke in hushed tones.

'It's obvious,' she said, 'that if they're preparing some sort of general selection this time, neither children nor the elderly will be spared. And if they're taking us all for liquidation, we might as well wait for it here and be saved the ordeal of getting there. And suppose,' she mused out loud, 'that they really are sending us to labour camps. Then too the children won't be allowed to come along. I'm staying here,' she decided. 'Who knows the hiding place besides G.?'

'No one,' answered Stella.

'What will you do?' Sofia looked her in the eyes. 'Stella, think it over. Here none of us may get out alive, and there you'll still have a chance. Maybe Vilek's still alive in prison.'

'Prison or no prison, I'm staying here,' Stella declared.

'What will we do with Mother?' Sofia worried. 'She can't possibly hide with us up there with her asthma and coughing attacks.'

The two women rose and went to the spare room at the back that was built out of wood. Apparently it had once been used as a *sukkah* for the Jewish holidays.

'How do you get up there?'

'There's a ladder under the couch.' Stella bent over and pulled it out. 'It has to be stood on the bookcase. Do you see that slot in the ceiling? That's the keyhole. Yurik can go first and open it for us. The key should be here in this jar.'

The sound of people departing came from the yard below. Yurik stood in the doorway. 'Mama, everyone's leaving,' he said.

Stella looked down at the yard. 'The Rosenbergs are going too. There'll hardly be a soul left.'

An unceasing noise of footsteps came from the street.

Sofia called Yurik. 'Go on up,' she told him. 'You'll be in charge of opening and closing. Yes, just you,' she promised.

The old woman stayed below, in a ruined wing of the house that had been demolished during the German bombardments. She could lie there on some mattresses under a broken table. There was no question of her being able to manage in the cramped space of the dark loft. A coughing attack during a search could endanger them all. And the roof tiles couldn't be lifted for her either, because that might be seen from the yard. Besides which, she herself, quite simply, wanted to remain below.

Stella lay on her side with her eyes shut. Sofia sat in the middle, the one spot where it was possible to straighten up, and arranged the provisions they had brought with them.

A few rays of wan light strayed through the narrow opening between the walls and the roof. The two boys took advantage of them to lie reading some Sherlock Holmes novels that they had found in a dusty bundle in the attic.

'Are you going to let them read like that in the dark?'

'Why not, it's better that they read now than fight.'

The last people left the courtyard. For a while a few stragglers could still be heard in the street, but by noon they too were all gone. A deathly silence descended.

The next day there was only one noteworthy event. A man's heavy, shuffling footsteps were heard on the street and his shaking voice cried out: 'Mania! Mania! Mania!' The echo blended with his receding steps and then fell still.

The day after that the two women left the hiding place to gather what food had been left behind in the neighbouring apartments. The old woman emerged from the ruins to greet them.

'It seems to me,' she said, 'that I'm more comfortable where I am than you are up there. God grant that it all ends well.'

Sofia surveyed their loot. 'It will keep the five of us going for two weeks at the most,' she said. 'Then we'll go up to the top floor, hold hands, and jump into the air like angels.'

Stella knew she was not joking. The old woman went back to her mattress and the two of them returned to the hiding place with the food. Yurik pulled up the ladder and closed the trap door behind them.

Sofia lay staring at the two boys. 'Tell me,' she asked suddenly in full seriousness, 'does either of you understand what's happening, what our situation is here?'

'I do,' said Yurik confidently.

'So do I,' repeated Kazik after him.

On the morning of the third day the sound of footsteps made the four of them sit up. Someone entered the courtyard and stopped. The silence fell again and then suddenly a woman's voice was heard singing. She was singing a Jewish melody. It was sad, like most Jewish melodies. Her voice rose and spread poignantly through the empty apartments. She continued to sing, the barely audible catch in her throat ascending from the empty courtyard, around which stood the houses, the streets, the walled ghetto, the entire city of Warsaw.

Sofia brushed the tears from her eyes. 'She's gone mad,' she whispered, rising to push up the roof tiles and look down. Stella restrained her. 'Don't,' she said. 'It could be a trap.'

'Stella, what's the matter with you?'

But Stella insisted.

'There are men on the roof,' Yurik whispered. They heard footsteps on the roof tiles and a babble of voices.

'Woman,' somebody shouted. 'What happened at Mila? Hey there, woman! Where are you coming from? Hey!'

Policemen and soldiers burst into the courtyard. Sofia froze in astonishment. 'It's satanic, satanic,' she whispered. She shut her eyes and listened to them running up the stairs and onto the roof. She heard the men scream as they were dragged away.

G's voice could be made out in the yard, shouting orders. The door of their apartment burst open and someone came down the hallway.

'Pani Kosowolska!'

Stella recognized the voice. 'That's his assistant.'

'Pani Kosowolska! If you don't come out of your hiding

place on your own, we'll have to pull you out.'

Sofia didn't open her eyes. She heard the old woman climbing out from among the ruins. She heard her passing beneath them and saying a single word :

'*Shoyn.*'

Then came the sound of her slippers shuffling down the stairs.

And a shot.

The soldiers and policemen left the yard. It was silent once again.

The authorities allotted an area smaller than before for the survivors. The ghetto committee tried to organize life afresh. The factories that employed about a third of the remaining population were now situated like islands outside the ghetto walls. Of half a million Jews or more, perhaps a tenth were left. You could increase that figure a little if you counted those who had managed to hide on the Polish side, or to jump from the railway-wagons on their way.

8

'She always had high blood pressure,' said Doctor Wolff.

Stella took the towel from his hand. 'She was already unconscious when I tried to wake her this morning.'

The doctor bent over Sofia again. 'It looks to me as if the whole left side is affected,' he said.

'Just last night I asked her not to give all her supper to the two boys,' Stella told him. 'She had taken to doing that lately, but I might as well have talked to the wall. She even tried joking and said : "Well, if I go the boys will still have you." '

The doctor gathered his instruments and put them back in his bag. Stella helped him on with his coat. 'Thank you very much, doctor,' she said.

'There's nothing to thank me for. Poor Mitek. Not everyone's lucky enough to have had such a wife. Take care of yourself, Pani Stella.'

He met Yurik at the door. 'Ah, there you are, young man. Don't worry. Everything will be all right. Your mother will go to the hospital and come back again in good health.'

The doctor left. Stella put on her work smock. 'I have to go to the factory,' she told Yurik. She put a chair by Sofia's bed and said : 'Sit here and watch over your mother. When the ambulance comes I'll return.'

'What about Kazik?' he asked.

'It's best if he remains in the hiding place. And you, too. If you hear anyone in the yard, go right up and shut the trap door.'

Stella left and Yurik remained sitting by his mother. An hour went by. He decided that she must need to urinate. He took a pot, picked up the blanket, and shoved it underneath her. Sofia was wearing only her nightgown. Yurik looked at her legs and her stomach. He hadn't imagined that was how she looked. He covered her and sat down on the chair again. Perhaps she will die, he thought. He should keep something of hers for a remembrance. He took a pair of scissors from the drawer of the desk and bent down over her head. If only she doesn't open her eyes now, he prayed, snipping off a lock of her hair. That was enough, he decided. More might be noticed. It seemed to him that she stirred.

'Mama?'

No, she simply lay there, very pale, without moving.

'Yurik?' Kazik left the hiding place and came down to the room. 'What's wrong with Mama?'

'She's sick. Aunt Stella said you should wait in the hiding place until the ambulance comes.'

Kazik stood in the doorway for a minute, then turned around and went back.

Yurik took the pack of cards from the table and went through it. For a mother, he decided, it should be a queen. He folded the card in two and slipped the lock of hair inside it.

An ambulance entered the yard. Two orderlies came and took the sick woman. Stella accompanied them.

'It's too bad Aunt Anna isn't still at the hospital,' she said. 'Go and call Kazik.'

'Kazik!' he called. 'Come on. They're taking Mama.'

The orderlies transferred Sofia to a stretcher, raised it, and started down the stairs with her. 'Don't you know that you have to take a patient downstairs with his head up?' Stella hissed at them. 'Turn around!'

'We can't turn around now, Pani,' they apologized. 'We'll be down below in a minute.'

Kazik and Yurik climbed on the windowsill. They saw the orderlies put the stretcher in the van. The doctor closed the doors. The ambulance started up and backed around to leave the yard. Yurik climbed down and pulled up a chair to the other window that looked out on the street. The three of us stood on it.

I knew that Sofia wouldn't return.

Yurik looked out.

Kazik waved at the vanishing ambulance. 'Goodbye, Mama,' he called.

9

A workday towards evening.

People came home from the factory and began making supper. A long queue stood by the gate outside the grocery store. A yellow, long-legged dog chased after a cat. It caught it by the entrance to the neighbouring courtyard.

Yurik and Kazik stood on the concrete fence of what had once been a garden. The dog bit the cat and it yowled. The dog backed away and began to dance around it, filling the yard with its barks. The cat stiffened and prepared to defend itself with its claws, waving a paw at the dog whenever it got too close. Yurik and Kazik didn't budge. The dog bit the cat a second time, and then a third. The cat sat down defencelessly and the dog bit it again. Yurik threw a stone at it. The cat died and the dog went away. The doorman picked up the dead animal by the tail and threw it in the garbage. Kazik had tears in his eyes.

'I feel awfully sorry for it,' said Yurik.

Stella opened the window and called down: 'Yurik, get in the queue and get our bread, do you hear? Come over here, I'll throw you down the purse.'

Yurik went over to the window and she threw down the purse, which fell to the cobblestoned yard with a thud.

Following the Mila Street action, Stella had managed to get new numbers for herself and Sofia through Pan G. Yurik took over his mother's work number. Stella taught him to work at the looms. He worked with her in Pan Finkel's department. Kazik spent the day by their side, hiding behind the bundles of wool under Stella's loom during inspections. At first it was hard for Yurik to fill his daily quota, and Pan Finkel had to add to it in his production report, making up the difference from the output of the more experienced workers. After a while, though, Yurik learned to keep up and to meet the quota by himself. Once he was even credited with a new record, but Aunt Stella explained to him that this was merely to increase his standing with the management.

Sofia still lay in the hospital, but she was getting better. The doctors, most of them old friends of her husband, did their utmost to help. Yurik came to visit her only once. It was already winter.

'Are you glad to be seeing your mother? You're being asked a question!'

'Yes.'

Stella shook her head pityingly. 'Don't drag your feet on the pavement. I don't have a lifetime's supply of shoes for you. Forward march.' She pushed him through the gate of the hospital.

Yurik climbed the stairs ahead of her. She steered him into one of the corridors and put her hand on a door handle. 'It's right here. Say hello when you go in.' She opened the door. Yurik remained standing on the threshold.

A pale woman with a moustache lay on a bed in the bright, narrow room and looked at him with his mother's eyes. Then she smiled. 'Yurik, come over here, don't you recognize me? Are you frightened of the moustache? When I'm better you won't see it any more.' She opened her left hand a little. 'Look!' She kicked off the blanket with her right foot and waggled her left one a bit. 'Soon your mother will be well again and will come home. Why don't you smile at all, Yurik?'

Yurik said nothing.

A while later they said goodbye from across the room. 'I'm sorry I can't give you a kiss. There are all kinds of infectious diseases in a hospital. I'll see you soon, Yurik.'

Stella took him by the hand and they left the room

together. Downstairs he grabbed her by the sleeve. 'Aunt Stella!'

'What is it?' She stopped and looked around her. 'Holy mother!' she exclaimed. 'It's Pani Panska!'

She opened her purse and handed him several notes. 'Give these to her, but try not to let her see you. Go on now.'

Yurik went up to her and put the money in the plate by her chair. She didn't notice him. She had her head down and was absorbed in her bow as it rose and fell on her violin.

'She's playing, Aunt Stella.'

She took his hand. 'Come quick,' she said.

Pan Finkel left his office and strode on squeaky shoes through the work room. The workers stood by their machines, attending to the threads that wrapped themselves quickly around the spools. Pan Finkel liked the rhythmic hum of the machines. He had been born in a large industrial town with a caul around his head for good luck, which an ignorant midwife had thoughtlessly thrown away. Before the war he had been the manager of a large textile factory, and upon coming to Warsaw a year ago with his wife and son he had proposed to K. G. Schultz, whose plant was just being established, that he put together a spinning department for him from the odds and ends lying around in the yard. His proposal was accepted and carried out. Though his wife and son had been registered as non-deportables in recognition of his industrial success, the two were taken away one day at the very hour that he had gone to renew the stamps on their documents. With an escort of policemen he had gone from car to car of the train full of deportees from the *Umschlagplatz* without finding them. For weeks on end he roamed the factory half-mad, an evil spirit bottled up inside him, taking it out on his workers. It was then that Stella befriended him and succeeded in winning his heart. She would invite him over for dinner and go to tidy up his apartment. Yurik and Kazik admired his elegant handwriting.

'Look, Aunt Stella.'

'I see,' she said, glancing at the left-hand corner of the oilcloth that covered their table.

Stella Kosowolska
Viktor Finkel

'Good morning, Pan Finkel,' Yurik greeted him while splicing together a torn thread.

Viktor Finkel nodded in acknowledgment. 'How's the work going?'

'Fine, Pan Finkel. I'm really good at it now.'

'Go to your aunt now,' said the manager. 'Someone else will take your place today. She wants to send you somewhere.'

Yurik stopped the machine and went over to Stella.

'Pan Finkel sent me to you.'

'Yes, I know. You're to go today with Pan Adam and Pan Altertum to get coal for us,' she told him.

'Who's Pan Altertum?'

'You'll find out in a minute. Here they come. Pan Adam has a sack for you too. Behave yourself and pay attention to what he tells you.'

'Is the boy ready? How are you, Stella?'

'Fine, he's all yours,' she smiled back.

Pan Adam pinched his cheek. 'You'll be a treasure-hunting hero today,' he said.

The three of them crept through a hidden opening

behind the wool shelves. Pan Adam led them over rooftops, up staircases and into attics, through strange, empty apartments and holes in walls that connected one house with another.

'Here we are,' he said, pointing to a large mountain landscape hanging on a wall. 'This is the house.'

He moved the picture aside to uncover a gap in the wall. Yurik clambered through it first. 'It's pitch dark in here,' he called back.

'Don't worry,' Pan Adam answered. 'Let's go, Altertum, it's your turn now.'

The light that shone through the opening was suddenly blocked by Altertum's large, hunched frame. It struggled there for a while and stopped.

'What's happened?' asked Pan Adam.

'I can't get through,' answered Altertum.

'Then come back out and try again.'

Altertum resumed his contortions.

'Adam, I can't come out either.'

Yurik heard Pan Adam curse heartily on the other side of the wall. Bits of plaster and broken brick began to fall from the opening. Yurik leaped to one side to avoid being crushed by the man, who suddenly fell into the corridor with his arms and legs outspread. Pan Adam jumped in after him. 'Let's go,' he commanded. Altertum got to his feet and smoothed out his clothes.

They groped their way down a long hallway, bumping repeatedly into the furniture that had been piled along the walls. Altertum kept tripping and knocking things over, but he managed to keep up with them. Pan Adam opened a door and they entered a large, well-furnished apartment that was flooded with winter light. Pan Adam halted suddenly and signalled them to be quiet. Footsteps could be heard on the stairs. 'It must be German inspectors,' he whispered. 'Go back to the entrance and wait for me there.' Altertum ran back down the corridor, knocking over the furniture. Yurik ran after him. Pan Adam stayed by the door.

'You can come back,' he called. 'He's gone away. It must have been someone like us.' Yurik and Altertum returned to the apartment. Pan Adam was standing by the window.

'You needn't be afraid, whoever you are,' he called down to someone below.

A Pole with a coachman's cap was standing in the courtyard, about to flee through the gate. In his arms he held a stack of china dishes, which he balanced with his chin. 'Holy Mary, you scared me! I nearly broke everything. What are you looking for up there?'

'Coal,' said Pan Adam. 'Have you seen any coal?'

'Try down below,' said the man in the courtyard. 'I thought you were the Germans.' He turned and disappeared through the gate.

Yurik stood by a desk and read the title page of a book: Jules Verne, *Twenty Thousand Leagues Under the Sea.* He began to leaf through a stamp album lying near it. Pan Altertum stood by the wardrobe.

'What did you find?' Pan Adam asked him.

'Nothing,' he answered, removing some dresses and coats from their hangers and draping them over his arm.

'Is this your idea of coal?' Pan Adam asked him. 'I'm not going back with you with all that stuff. You can find your way yourself.'

Pan Altertum thought it over before regretfully laying everything on the table.

'Yurik, get a move on,' Pan Adam called to him. 'We haven't got much time.'

'I'm coming,' he answered. He slipped two books under his sweater and hurried out.

They descended to a ground-floor apartment. Pan Adam debated for a moment which door to open and then chose the left one. He stopped short in the doorway, causing Pan Altertum, who was hurrying after, to collide with him. Squeezed between them, Yurik craned his neck and peeped into the room. Around a table spread with a white cloth and set with expensive dishes and silver sat nine people, men, women and children, their heads on their chests or propped against the table. Not one of them moved.

'They're dead,' Yurik whispered.

Pan Altertum raised his eyes to the ceiling and sighed piteously. Pan Adam pushed them both out of the doorway and closed the door softly. 'May they rest in peace,' he said. 'I was here just the day before yesterday,' he marvelled. 'They must have been hiding in here all the time.' He turned and looked at Yurik. 'We're old men already,' he said. 'If you live, remember what you've seen. It's up to you to remember.'

Everyone in Sofia's family was taken from her father's home in Czestochow except himself. The old man wished to end his life sitting in the green armchair in his library, and a German *Unteroffizier* kindly obliged him.

Sofia never learned of her family's fate. In January the authorities once more set about thinning out the population of the ghetto. The deportation lasted three days. The ghetto dwellers had spent the autumn preparing well-made shelters stocked with provisions in which they now took refuge. In the course of the action the entire hospital, doctors and patients together, was moved out and shipped eastward.

Sofia went straight to heaven. By the entrance she met her brother Edek.

Soshka, he said, happy to see her, tell the truth, wouldn't

it have been better if you'd had a little vial of cyanide too? How long they dragged you about down there!

Don't talk about it, she begged him, still under the influence of events down below. Some day I'll prove to you that I was right in spite of everything.

How are the boys? asked Edek.

Oh my, Sofia remembered. I forgot to tell Stella that Yurik has a big cavity in one of his molars. It slipped my mind completely.

Edek smiled. Come, he said, let's go in.

Arm in arm, sister and brother disappeared behind a boulevard of life-and-knowledge trees, which an angel was in the middle of watering. Sofia didn't even notice that she had suddenly sprouted wings.

'He asked me how many dresses I was wearing. I looked him straight in the eye, and said one.'

'You always have such good luck, Pani Stella,' smiled the neighbour. 'Yesterday they shot Kraszinska for doing the same.'

'At least the children will be looked after now,' Stella continued. 'All the jewels are already with Ella.'

'I'd like to know how you get away with it!' marvelled the neighbour.

'She has the face for it,' laughed Viktor. 'People believe her. Stella, you'll burn the boy's head off.'

'What can I do? This hydrogen peroxide just doesn't do a thing to his hair. It's as thick as a horse's mane.'

Kazik sat in front of her at the table while she tried to dye his hair blond. 'Just a little more, Kazhiula,' she promised. 'I can see you're being really brave. Yurik, turn on the light, it's getting dark.'

Yurik switched on the light and returned to watch his

brother at the table. Stella had begun to despair. 'I'm just not getting anywhere,' she said. 'And your grandparents had to go and have you both circumcised too! As though the sky would have fallen in if they hadn't. Now you'll pay for their fanaticism with your lives. Who told you to grow such hair, Kazhiula? Let me try it once more. Be patient for just a little longer,' she urged him.

'He's a redhead and always will be,' said Yurik, humming under his breath:

> *Your father's red, your mother's red,*
> *And a red priest the two of them wed.*

'You're a black Judas yourself!' Kazik retorted angrily.

'Sit quietly,' Stella soothed him, 'or else I'll burn your brains out. You're not a redhead at all. Any woman would be proud to have chestnut hair like yours. And such eyelashes,' she added.

> *Chestnut, chestnut, chestnut,*

sang Yurik. Kazik didn't react.

> *Lashes of chestnut, o lashes of chestnut.*

Kazik kept still. Yurik went down to the yard to sell his stamp collection to one of the boys. Tomorrow he was going over to the Polish side and he couldn't take it with him.

'Will you give me thirty-five crowns for it?'

'No, just thirty-two.'

'All right, give me thirty-two.'

'It's a deal?'

'A deal.'

They shook hands.

'Just don't go crying to your mother afterwards.'

'I won't.'

Yurik came back up from the yard. 'When is Kazik crossing over to the Polish side?'

'He'll come a day after you, or at the most two,' answered Stella.

Yurik examined his brother's hair. 'It's the same chestnut red as before.'

Kazik kept still.

'I've burned your brother's whole scalp, and nothing has happened to the hair. All right, that's the way it will have to be.'

'I've brought you some cigarettes as a present.'

'For me? Where did you get the money from? Thanks awfully. Who would have thought it! How did you get them?'

'I bought them in the store. With the money from selling my stamps.'

'Thank you very much,' said Stella again. She took out a cigarette and lit it.

Yurik crossed over to the Polish side the next day and safely reached the Catholic home that had agreed to take him in. The day after Kazik was returned by a sentry at the gate on the grounds that so small a child couldn't possibly be a labourer going to work.

Two days later a friend of Pan Finkel's, a *Volksdeutsch*, got Kazik out of the ghetto and brought him in a carriage to where Yurik was staying.

10

Formations of soldiers faced each other across the floor, taking cover in domino houses and bunkers of coloured blocks. Yurik and Kazik lay by their soldiers. Yurik took a coin and flicked it at his brother's troops. It fell among their ranks, leaving dead and wounded in its path.

'I killed Robin Hood!' Yurik exulted, jumping to his feet.

'That wasn't him.'

'You rotten liar, you said that the one without a bayonet was Robin Hood.'

'No, I didn't,' Kazik maintained.

Yurik threw down the soldier in his hand. 'I'm not playing with you any more,' he said, getting up again. 'You keep changing him from one to another to keep him alive. It's against the rules.'

'Don't play, then! I didn't change him.'

'All right, but remember.' Yurik returned to the game. 'It's my turn again. Watch. I'm firing at your capital.' He paused and rose on his elbows to listen to the footsteps coming up the stairs. 'Who's that coming?'

Kazik listened for a moment.

'Those are the quick footsteps that live across from us,' he said.

'She's back already,' said Yurik, surprised. 'All right, here goes,' he added in a lower voice.

'Pan Petrushka,' said the whiny voice of a woman from the staircase. 'Pan Petrushka, what's new in town?'

'Nothing's new,' the man's voice answered. 'Did you hear that Marishka's going with Yanek?'

'That's as old as the hills, Pan Petrushka, and with a beard on it.'

137

'And did you hear that they found some Jews over at Kowalska's place?'

'What are you telling me!' The woman was astonished. 'A good Catholic like her hiding Christ-killers? How's your daughter, Pan Petrushka?'

'Better, Pani, better. The doctor said she can get out of bed in a few days' time. Could you perhaps let me have the loan of a kilo of potatoes? My wife's coming back from the village tomorrow and we'll return them with interest.'

'She's talking to the shuffling steps down below,' said Yurik. 'I'm advancing. Take a good look so that you don't say I cheated.'

Captain Nemo had led Yurik's troops to the very wall of Kazik's capital. Thaddeus Kosciusko in person, mounted on a white horse, now charged from the flank at the head of a regiment of sabre-wielding cavalry that Yurik had drawn and cut out of cardboard. Tadek Swierczewski, his old friend from Zoliboz, joined the fray with a long column of reserves, horsemen and infantry, who advanced from position to position towards the front. General Boehm trotted on his horse before his batteries of cannon. Artillery, fire!

Victory was at hand. The walls of the capital crumbled before a barrage of heavy coins fired at close range. The last of Kazik's soldiers broke and ran for an isolated fortress at the far end of the floor. Yurik took the city and bombarded the fleeing defenders with their own guns. Three times he raked them with fire; three times they retreated the maximum distance, the width of Kazik's outspread hand. Only one of Kazik's soldiers was still alive, at a distance of one more hand from the fort. Yurik aimed and fired. The coin struck the soldier, who somersaulted in the air and landed again on his feet.

'He's still standing!' Kazik shouted.

'Let me have him, but remember where he was.

Don't move him.' Yurik turned the hero over and looked at his base. 'He already has two decorations,' he said. He took a pencil and drew a third cross next to them. 'He gets a name.'

'He's mine,' Kazik boasted. 'I'll call him . . . Ironhand.'

'I've already reserved that,' Yurik protested. 'I read the book first.'

'No, you didn't.'

'All right,' he conceded. 'But it's your go.'

'Ironhand gallops off on his horse,' Kazik said.

'He doesn't have a horse,' declared Yurik.

'Yes he does. Don't interrupt me.'

Yurik fired.

'Missed!'

Ironhand reached the gates of the fort and vanished inside. Yurik staged a massive assault. Cavalry, foot soldiers and horse-drawn artillery poured forth from every direction. Colourful regiments formed a broad arc in front of the fortress walls. The heroes of novels, famous generals, and the bearers of titles Yurik had invented led his forces against the enemy's last stronghold. Ironhand faithfully deployed his three cannon and shelled his attackers with each in turn, but still they drew nearer. Lead and paper soldiers, pistol bullets and rifle cartridges, queens, bishops and chess pawns, stood at the foot of the fort.

'Surrender!'

'Ironhand never surrenders!'

'Let me have him, I'm taking him prisoner.'

'You'll have to find him. He's hiding.'

'Liar, you've got him in your pocket!' Yurik fell on his brother, struggling to get the soldier. Kazik fought as hard as he could. Yurik twisted his hand and discovered the fugitive in his clenched fist.

Kazik was close to tears. 'Give him back!'

'No, he's my prisoner. My men are marching him back to me. On your knees, coward! Beg for your life from the Commander of the Universe, Jan Grenadier Tarzan. Ironhand is thrown to the floor and I personally slap him in the face.' Yurik cut the air forcefully with his hand. 'Off to the dungeon!' he commanded.

Kazik's eyes filled with tears at the injustice done to his hero. He threw himself in despair at his brother, trying to get Ironhand back. 'Let me have him,' he sobbed.

Yurik fought free and ran laughing around the table. Kazik ran after him, crying unrestrainedly. 'Let me have him, you pig!'

'Idiot, don't cry so loud. The neighbours'll hear us.'

Kazik restrained his sobs. Yurik began to feel sorry for Ironhand. 'All right,' he said. 'Do you agree to my executing him with full honours and then we'll fight another war?'

'Yes,' Kazik agreed.

Yurik leaned the prisoner against his fort and stood a squad of marksmen opposite him under the command of General Gordon of Khartoum.

'I'm tying his hands and eyes.'

'You don't have to blindfold him,' said Kazik bravely.

'What's your last wish?'

'To have this letter delivered to my wife.'

The soldiers shouldered their rifles.

'Wait, drums,' Kazik reminded him.

The drummers beat out a roll on their drums.

'Long live Poland the free and invincible!' cried Ironhand.

'Fire!' ordered General Gordon.

The rifles rang out. Ironhand still leaned against the wall, his head fallen on his breast.

'Do you want to give him a funeral?'

But Kazik had stopped playing and was listening to the stairs. 'Christina's coming.' He knew her steps. 'She's bringing lunch.'

A blonde, trim girl of about eighteen entered the room carrying a laundry basket and a bouquet of lilacs.

'See what I brought you? It's spring outside. The lilac's in bloom.' She put the flowers in a vase and filled it with water from the pitcher. 'I'm in an awful rush, because my mother has lots of laundry today. Hurry up and eat,' she requested. She removed the washing from the basket and handed them the plates of food that were underneath it.

'Kazik's been crying,' she said, studying his face.

'We were just playing a game,' explained Yurik. 'Can you exchange books for us?'

'Have you already finished the ones I brought you? I'll bring you new ones tomorrow,' she promised. 'I've got you some coloured paper, and some cardboard and glue. I'll bring it all up tonight. I had nowhere to put it now.'

The boys finished eating and Christina returned the plates to the basket.

'Don't forget to change the water in the vase every day. It's a shame to let them wilt right away.' She took the basket and left.

'Ready for more?' asked Yurik.

'Let's have some peacetime first.'

'And then we'll play war again?'

'Yes, but later.'

Christina went down to the laundry.

QUICK AND CLEAN said the sign on the window at the front of the house. Christina, her mother, and two hired girls did the wash inside amid vaporous clouds of steam. Pani Sadomska, whose husband had been killed fighting in the defence of Warsaw, had agreed to take in the two Jewish boys in return for a handsome fee. Her own two-room apartment was attached to the laundry by a narrow corridor. She and her daughter lived in one of the rooms, and her sixteen-year-old son in the other. The room in which the two boys were hidden was seven flights up on the roof.

'There won't be any bill collectors here,' Pani Sadomska had warned them when they arrived. 'Don't open the door for anyone. Whenever we come we'll give three knocks three times. And try to be quiet. It's our luck that no one's living underneath you.'

The thick wooden beam supporting the ceiling made the room look like a peasant cottage. The furniture was simple and very old. There were two broad wooden beds, a two-legged easy chair that rested against the wall with its springs sticking out, and a wobbly table that must have dated from Napoleon's time. A curtain serving as a partition between the room and the washing area, in which stood a sink, a pitcher of water and a bucket, completed the scene. Two pictures adorned the walls, one of Jesus bearing his cross through the streets of Jerusalem, and the other of Saint Peter. By them hung a drawing, clipped apparently from an advertisement, of a sailboat on a lake.

'It's getting too dark to see anything,' said Kazik.

'Let's put everything away.' They threw all the toys in a chest and pushed it under a bed. They lay down next to each other and waited for their supper.

'Tadek's coming with her,' announced Kazik.

Yurik went to open the door. Christina lit the kerosene lamp and started preparing the table. Tadek sat on a bed and followed a fly buzzing on the window pane with his watery expressionless eyes. He suddenly leaped up, crushed it against the glass, and returned to the bed again.

Christina liked talking with Yurik. She had never gone beyond the fourth grade and was amazed by how much he knew and thought. Her brother, who had been brain-damaged in infancy by a fall from his crib, had never even finished first grade.

If what Yurik said was true, Christina mused, the stars were really very strange. But what kept them burning all the time? He had told her something else too . . . oh, yes: about the Greeks who had died defending a narrow pass in the mountains. She remembered that they had written something on the stone walls of the pass. It was a nice story. She had tried telling it to Zbishek, but such things didn't interest him. 'Let's dance,' he had said.

'Will you marry him?' asked Yurik.

'I don't know. Maybe.'

'Christina,' whispered Yurik. 'Look what's happened to Tadek.'

Tadek, who had been sitting quietly on the corner of the bed, suddenly waved his hands spastically and keeled over with his eyes wide open. Christina rushed over, grabbed him by the arms, and began to drag him around the room. 'Tadek,' she cried, 'wake up! Tadek!'

Tadek woke up and stood on his feet. 'What happened?' he asked.

Christina calmed down. 'It happens to him sometimes,' she explained to the boys. 'Afterwards he never remembers a thing. It's because the blood goes to the wrong place in his brain.'

Tadek helped her collect the plates and pack the basket. 'It's already late,' said Christina. 'Good night.'

Yurik lowered the wick of the lamp and lay down in bed. The silence around them was broken at intervals by the sound of hoofbeats or the horn of a passing car.

'Kazik, do you want to play submarines?'

Yurik got out of bed and put the kerosene lamp under the table.

'Hang up your blanket too,' he said to Kazik as he

143

draped his own from the table top. The two of them crawled under it and sat there on pillows. Yurik turned up the lamp.

'Captain Nemo! Full speed ahead! We're heading for Treasure Island.'

Afterwards they sat on the table and looked out over the dim rooftops at the stars. 'The moon was on that side of the chimney before,' Yurik showed his brother, 'and now it's on the other side. Do you see? That means that the earth is really turning around.'

The full moon rose over the pitch of the roof and looked into their room.

'It has a face,' said Yurik. 'Look carefully.'

'It's a little cross-eyed,' said Kazik.

Yurik awoke in the middle of the night. The lamp had nearly gone out. Someone tall and dark was standing in the corner of the room. Yurik strained to hear. A floorboard creaked by the door. Someone had come in through the shut door. The board creaked again. Someone was approaching his bed, coming nearer and nearer without touching it.

'Kazik.'

'I'm not asleep.'

'I'll give you ten free commands if you get up now and turn up the lamp.'

'I can't,' replied Kazik.

'I'll give you General Gordon too,' said Yurik.

'I can't.'

'If I turn it up myself will you come and sleep with me?'

'Yes,' Kazik agreed.

Yurik quickly threw back the blanket from over his head and reached the lamp with a single bound. The shadows vanished. Kazik crossed over to his bed.

'But no kicking, and no pulling the blanket.'

'It's always you who pulls.'

The lamp went out by itself. Yurik and Kazik fell asleep, huddled together in the moonlight.

Strange footsteps mounted the stairs and stopped outside their door. The two of them listened tensely. The knocker knocked three times and three times again. It stopped.

'Should I open it?' asked Yurik in a whisper.

The knocker knocked three more times.

'That's nine. I'm going to open it.'

A large stranger wearing a stiff, round hat entered the room. He looked at them and then looked for a place to hang his hat. In the end he put it by his briefcase on the table and sat down in the easy chair.

'Good morning, boys,' he said. He smiled at Kazik and raised his chin. 'What's your name, young man?'

Kazik didn't answer.

'His name is Kazimierz Stefan Kosopolski,' Yurik answered for him.

'Be quiet!' the stranger said angrily. 'I wasn't aware that anyone had asked you.' He smiled again at Kazik. 'Where did you live before coming here, young man?'

Kazik sat there bewildered. He couldn't for the life of him remember the complicated story he had been instructed to tell under such circumstances.

'We're from Lvov,' Yurik said.

Sergeant Zuk wheeled around and slapped him in the face. 'I asked you not to answer for him,' he warned. 'Are you Jewish?' he asked Kazik.

Kazik's bewilderment grew, but he shook his head.

'He isn't,' said Yurik.

The sergeant spun around again. 'Wiseguy! I told you

to shut up. Do you hear me?'

'He . . . he doesn't talk so well,' Yurik apologized. 'He's still little.'

'Are you Jewish?' This time the question was finally directed at Yurik.

'No.'

'What's your name?'

'Jerzy Henryk Kosopolski. We're Pani Sadomska's nephews. We came here from Lvov because the Russians were there. They killed our father and mother, and we were sent here by our uncles.'

'You took the train to Warsaw?'

'Yes.'

'And then?'

'We took a carriage.'

'Did the driver have a moustache?'

'It was a long time ago,' said Yurik.

'How do you like Warsaw, better than Lvov?'

Yurik forgot himself. 'Oh, yes,' he said. 'Warsaw's much nicer. Especially Zoliboz.'

'The train went through Zoliboz?'

'Yes,' Yurik replied, giving himself away.

'Oh,' said the sergeant.

Christina came with their afternoon snack and paused pale-faced in the doorway. The sergeant gave them a last look. 'Oh well,' he said. He took his briefcase and his hat. 'Goodbye, boys,' he said.

The two boys waited wordlessly for him to leave. Christina followed him out. He locked the door from outside and removed the key.

'He took it,' whispered Yurik. They waited for the footsteps to disappear from the yard and lay down on one of the beds.

'What's going to happen?'

146

Yurik shrugged.

'Nothing's going to happen,' Kazik suddenly said.

'How do you know?'

'I had a dream.'

'What did you dream?'

'Brown Suit and Grey Suit came to the door and threatened us with pistols. Not real pistols, ones like ours. They were even made out of cardboard, and were flat.'

'So?'

'We ran down some streets with Aunt Ella until we got here. Then the ceiling opened up and a naked man came out with lots of hair. There was a lot of light and he had a cross. I think it must have been Jesus.'

'When did you dream it?'

'The night before last.'

'You're not making it up? Swear to me.'

'I swear,' Kazik promised.

'Swear by Papa.'

'I swear by Papa.'

'Then what happened?'

'They got smaller and disappeared into the floor. You know,' Kazik remembered, 'Pani Sadomska said that when we become Catholics after the war Christina will be our godmother.'

'Should we pray?' asked Yurik.

Kazik nodded.

'Hail Mary, full of grace,' Yurik began.

'Full of grace,' Kazik repeated after him.

'Pray for us now and at the hour of our death, Amen.'

Sergeant Zuk of the secret police informed his superiors that his investigation had confirmed that two children were staying with Pani Sadomska, as a certain tenant in the house had reported, but that the boys were undoubtedly the lady's Catholic nephews who had come from Lvov.

Ella obtained his address and went to thank him. She offered him money but he refused. In token of her appreciation she sent him a present of considerable value together with a large bouquet of white lilies.

A bomb fell. Yurik and Kazik sat in the darkness on the table in their room. 'Give us this day our daily bread,' they prayed. The walls of the room shook and a window pane shattered from the explosion. 'Forgive us our trespasses as we forgive those who trespass against us.'

'I'm scared,' whispered Kazik.

'It's the Russians,' Yurik reassured him. 'Look, you can see the anti-aircraft fire.'

'Let's lie down and pray some more,' Kazik suggested.

Yurik lay down next to him and Kazik wrapped his arms around him. There was another explosion.

'Do you know the Credo by heart?'

'No, but I'll say it after you.'

'I believe,' Yurik began, 'in God the omnipotent Father, Creator of heaven and earth.'

A majestic pageant of aerial warfare filled the night sky.

11

Anna had managed to acquire the papers of a woman who had died several years previously in eastern Galicia and to make the necessary changes in them. She lived with her daughter in the house of a family of destitute Polish

148

nobility who suspected nothing. Yoasha attended the local school like any child her age. Her mother was in town on some business and the girl sat at the dining-room table doing her lessons. In the doorway of his father's room stood the family's youngest son, a boy of Yoasha's age, arguing heatedly with the old man.

'Come here, you rotten little bastard! What did you say?'

'Are you deaf? It stinks in your room, I'm staying out here.'

'Just wait, just wait,' the old man threatened. 'Wait until your mother comes home.'

Yanek took a step towards his father's bed. 'I'm earning good money,' he shouted, raising his voice as loud as he could.

The old man cupped his hand to his ear.

'We stand near the ghetto,' Yanek continued to shout. 'When someone comes by looking like a kike, we grab him. Hand over your cash, we tell him, or we'll kick your arse right to the police.'

The old man fell back on his pillow and lay there with his eyes shut. Then he got out of bed, stuck his feet in a pair of slippers, and walked in the direction of the bathroom, lacing his pants as he went. He passed Yoasha, gave the key in the front door a sudden turn, took down the coachman's whip that hung on the wall, and swung it at his son. Yanek leaped from his place and took cover behind Yoasha. The old man ran panting after him, trying to land a second blow. The boy managed to grab the end of the whip and to jerk it from his father's shaking hands.

'Give it back!' the old man grumbled.

'Over your dead body!'

'I say give it back, you bastard!'

Yanek laughed. The old man returned to his bed and lay down.

'You're not leaving the house,' he said.

'I wasn't intending to.'

The old man was silent. Then he called to his son in a less truculent voice.

'What do you want?'

'Come here.'

'Are you going to hit me?'

'No.'

Yanek approached him.

'Didn't you help the partisans to blow up the railway tracks?'

'Sure I did,' the boy said proudly.

'And wasn't one of them a Jew?'

'Yes, he was.'

'And who's killing off all our Jews?'

'The Krauts, who do you think!'

'So a Pole like you wants to help the Germans do their work, eh?'

'They're kikes,' Yanek said in self-defence.

'They're kikes!' the old man roared, rising on his elbows. 'They're Polish kikes, you son of a bitch! When we have our Polish republic again we'll do with them as we like. But now there isn't any republic and there aren't any kikes; there are only Poles and Germans. Get out of this house, you Judas Iscariot, right now!' He reached out to throw the boy the key, but his aim was amiss and it fell back down on the bed. The old man turned to the wall and curled up in his blanket, cursing silently to himself. Yanek went to pick up the key. 'Why don't you learn to throw first,' he said.

The old man didn't answer.

'What a character, huh?' Yanek sought Yoasha's support.

Yoasha didn't look up from her book. 'I'm not talking to you today,' she said.

'Oh, so you're going to be a Jew like him. Don't talk

then, goddamn it!' Yanek left the room, slamming the door behind him.

The noise roused the old man. 'Now go and plaster the ceiling, you lousy bastard!' he shouted after him.

Yanek went down the stairs, whistling happily to himself. Yoasha continued her homework.

There was a knock on the door. 'Yoasha, open up.' It was Anna. 'Is Pani Raymond here?'

'No, she went to sell the coats that Yanek brought from the ghetto.'

'Come into the kitchen, I have something to tell you. Yurik and Kazik have moved to a new hiding place in the country.'

'What happened?'

'A family of *Volksdeutsch* moved into the apartment beneath them. Has the water boiled yet?'

'Yes,' said Yoasha.

Anna poured herself a cup of tea. 'Pani Sadomska,' she continued, 'was very pleased with the boys and was sorry to see them go. She told me that Yurik came back up the stairs especially to kiss her hand.'

'What an idiot,' Yoasha declared. 'He has no pride.'

Anna smiled. 'What do you know about it! Go and run yourself a bath. I'll be in in a minute.'

Yoasha put down her book and went to the bathroom, locking the door behind her. Anna finished her tea and followed after. 'Yoashka,' she said, 'let me in. Yoashka, don't you hear me?'

'I don't want to,' the girl said.

'Why, what's the matter?' Anna asked, astonished.

'I don't want to! I'm busy washing now.'

Anna considered for a moment. 'I'm asking you to open the door,' she said in anger. 'I still have to get to town today.'

'I'm not opening it,' Yoasha insisted crossly. 'It's embarrassing to wash with you here.'

'What? Very well, don't open it.' She suddenly burst out laughing. 'What a sillyhead you are!'

'Father?'

The old man awoke. 'Are you back, you little snot?'

Yanek handed him a note. 'Here's a hundred for you.'

'Where did you get it?'

'From a Jew.'

The old man crumpled the note in his hand as though to throw it in the boy's face. Yanek smiled. 'You'll never reach me. Anyway, I helped him.'

'You helped him what?'

'Escape.'

'And he gave it to you of his own free will?'

'You can see for yourself that he gave it to me.'

The old man put his hand under the blanket and took out the whip. 'Here, hang it back up,' he said. He picked up the note again, smoothed it out, and studied it with interest.

'Yanek.'

'What?'

The old man handed him the note. 'Run downstairs and buy me a fifth of vodka. But quick, before your mother gets back.'

12

'Hurry up! Get a move on!' the lead soldiers urged the group of deportees.

A volley of shots rang out from one of the coloured block houses. Three soldiers fell to the floor.

'Revolt!' shouted Kazik. 'Revolt!'

'That's against the rules,' Yurik protested, standing his soldiers back on their feet.

'Pan Petrushka, what do you say about our Jews now? It turns out that they know how to shoot too. It's no less than a third front.'

'Don't you worry, Pani, sooner or later each one of those little bugs will roast. The Lord be praised, we'll have a Jewless republic when this war is over.'

The Jews took up arms. The German army threw armoured units into the ghetto. Teams of sappers went about blowing up houses. SS troops were forced to advance rooftop by rooftop, alleyway by alleyway. Yurik and Kazik could see the smoke rising over the roofs from their window, and at night, the glow of the flames.

The turn of the K. G. Schultz factory came on the evening of the revolt's tenth day. Units of sappers poured kerosene all over the building. Trucks went back and forth, removing what could be salvaged from the warehouses. Schultz ran about the yard, urging on the Polish workers.

Stella and Viktor hid behind the medicine cabinet in the infirmary. Several wounded soldiers were brought in from a nearby street.

'Where's the key to the cabinet?' barked the medic.

'To hell with it!' snarled Schultz, kicking in the cabinet

door. It gave way. Stella squeezed Viktor's hand hard. The soldiers had their wounds dressed and were evacuated. Stella and Viktor ran upstairs to the Rosenbergs'.

'It's us, Finkel.'

'Climb up on the shelf over the door,' the Rosenbergs advised them from the pantry. Viktor climbed up first and helped Stella up after him.

'What are you waiting for?' asked Stella.

'We heard from one of the Poles that Schultz wants to blow up a section of the ghetto wall,' Pani Rosenberg said in a whisper. 'If he doesn't have to go the long way around, he can get more out of the warehouses. We'll go down as soon as we hear the explosions and try to get through the hole. There's nothing to lose any more.'

They listened in silence to the noise of the trucks and the shouts in the yard. A machine gun barked nervously in the distance, followed by the thump of grenades.

'Ours,' whispered Stella with tears in her eyes.

'There's no point in waiting any longer,' said Viktor suddenly. 'The whole building is liable to go up in flames at any minute.'

'Go and take a look, maybe you can see if they're about to blow up the wall.'

'That's easier said than done,' Viktor grumbled. 'Schultz is carrying on down in the yard with a pistol.'

'Then don't go,' Stella said angrily, swinging her legs off the shelf.

'Wait,' he stopped her, 'I'll go, I'll go.' He slipped off the shelf and went to the stairway. He approached the window gingerly and looked out, trying to show as little of himself as possible. Schultz was down in the yard. Two Ukranian soldiers stood behind his turned back while he looked at some documents. Viktor plucked up his nerve and leaned through the window to get a look at the gate.

Just then Schultz turned around and saw him. He pointed to him with the hand that was holding the papers. The soldiers lowered their rifles and ran towards the stairs. Viktor was brought to Schultz with his hands up.

'Herr Schultz,' he apologized, 'it's me, Finkel, who set up the spinning department. I haven't had time to leave the factory yet.'

'Who else is with you?' asked Schultz.

'Kosowolska and the Rosenbergs,' answered Viktor.

Schultz glanced at his watch. 'You're in luck,' he said. 'There's still time to make the last train.' He turned to one of the soldiers and snapped : 'Take them away. There are four of them.'

The soldier saluted. 'Shall I finish them off on the street, sir?'

'No,' said Schultz. 'Take them to the nearest *Umschlagplatz.*'

'Yes, sir.' He pointed his rifle at Viktor and marched him up the stairs.

'Everybody out!' he ordered from the doorway of the room.

Stella came down from the shelf and the Rosenbergs left the pantry. Pan Rosenberg was pale as a ghost. The soldier counted them.

'Let's go,' he said in Ukranian.

'What about our things?' said Viktor. 'We have to pack for the trip.'

The soldier stopped to think it over.

'They're taking us a long way,' said Viktor.

'All right,' he decided, 'you can pack a few things, but you only have five minutes. Do you have a watch on you, Jew? You keep track of the time.'

Viktor filled his knapsack with woollen socks, the only article of clothing in the room, while Stella slipped a bag of sugar and a bottle of water among her belongings.

'Viktor,' she said in a whisper, 'go and talk to him. Can't you see he's a stupid peasant who doesn't know his right hand from his left? I have my father's watch with me.'

The four of them shouldered their knapsacks. The men helped the women with the straps.

'Let's move,' said the soldier, pointing his rifle.

'Sergeant,' Viktor turned to him meekly, 'we have a gold watch, and there's five hundred crowns extra for you if you let us go now.'

'Let's move,' the soldier repeated.

'A gold watch with a chain, it's solid gold too.'

'Let's move,' said the soldier again, less confidently than before.

'And five hundred extra for drinks. Think it over, Sergeant. We're honest people and we stick to our word. God will bless you for the good deed.'

The soldier put down his rifle and scratched his bald pate perplexedly. 'But they told me to take you,' he said.

'How will they know if you took us or not? Let us go free on the street, wait a while and come back. No one will suspect you.'

'I have to bring back a paper with writing,' said the soldier.

'Who writes on it?' asked Viktor.

'One of our men.'

'He'll write it for you without us,' Viktor promised. 'He's sure to be a decent fellow, Sergeant, just like you. I'll even throw in another hundred so that you can treat him to a drink too.'

The soldier stood dumbly and laboriously ordered his thoughts, moving his lips now and then. In the end he shouldered his rifle. 'I'm going,' he said. 'Wait for me here.'

'Take a down payment,' Viktor suggested.

'No. I'll come back and take it all. A watch and a thousand crowns,' he said, 'and a gold chain too. Stay here until I come back.' He turned and left.

'Wheeew!' Pani Rosenberg exhaled.

'I've never seen the likes of it in my life,' said her husband. 'I hope he at least knows how to plough.'

'The idiot could have shot us all on the spot and taken everything,' said Viktor. 'Thank God he didn't have the brains for it.'

'Quiet,' Stella said to him. 'Don't give the devil ideas.'

At that very moment there was a tremendous explosion in the street. The four of them threw off their knapsacks and ran down to the yard. Trucks and wagons loaded with wool and clothing moved towards the hole in the wall. The Polish workers loaded them with the last bales. The Rosenbergs disappeared.

'Pretend you're loading,' whispered Viktor. He slipped a pair of socks into his trouser pocket and pretended to be one of the workers. Stella stuck close to him, holding on to the wagon. It reached the hole in the wall and the two of them vanished in smoke.

Pani Majewska opened the door and clapped her hands. 'Oh my God, it's the Jew! Who told you to come? We're not interested in hiding you any more. Take your money and get out of here.'

'Pani Majewska,' Viktor tried to coax her, 'let me in for a minute so we can talk. I think someone's coming up the stairs.'

'Well, then, hurry up.' She pulled him inside and shut the door. 'Jesus Christ!' she groaned. 'Marichna,' she called to someone in the next room, 'come and see the guest that's arrived.'

The door to the room opened and a thin, pale-faced girl stood staring at him from the doorway. Pani Majewska crossed her meaty arms on her breast and looked daggers at Viktor. 'Say what you have to say and then please go,' she declared.

'Perhaps you'll permit me to stay here until Pan Majewski comes back?' Viktor suggested. 'You understand, I have nowhere else to go. Everything's been burned to the ground. Here, here are some pairs of woollen socks for you, consider them a gift.'

The woman took the socks and inspected them. She put them on a stool by her side and waved her hand in acquiescence. 'Here, wait in the vegetable bin.' She opened a low door in the hallway for him. 'We'll see what Majewski has to say when he comes.'

Viktor crawled into the bin and lay down on the floor. He put a sack under his head and dozed off.

'Pan Jew?'

Viktor awoke with a start. 'Oh, it's you,' he said, calming down when he saw the girl looking in at him. 'What do you want?'

'I thought maybe you knew some arithmetic.'

'Arithmetic? Of course I know arithmetic. Bring me your notebook and I'll give you a hand.'

'No, you come out,' said the girl. 'It's too dark in there.'

Majewski came home from the market, opened the door to the bin, and began arranging the vegetables in it. Suddenly he stopped and cocked an ear.

Viktor's voice could be heard through the door of Marichna's room. 'One-half plus one-quarter, go on, write it down, equals three-quarters. Not that way! The three goes on top.'

'Stashka! Who's in there?'

His wife emerged from the kitchen, wiping her hands on her apron. 'The Jew came,' she said in low tones. 'He's teaching Marichna arithmetic.'

'Damn it all!' Majewski said angrily, banging his hat on the table. 'I thought they must have taken him away for sure by now.'

The days went by.

'Someone's coming!' whispered Pani Majewska in a frightened voice.

'Clear out,' said her husband between his teeth, 'quick!' Marichna opened the door for him and Viktor clambered out on the roof.

'You can come back,' she called. 'It was just some people visiting the neighbours.'

'It can't go on like this any more,' said Pan Majewski. 'You'll have to go somewhere else.'

'Who'll help me with my lessons?' complained the girl.

'You know what, Pan Majewski?' said Viktor. 'Make a false wall for me beneath the window and I'll lie in the space.'

Majewski agreed.

'What are you building there in your house, Majewski?' sniggered the neighbours. 'Every day you've got another brick under your coat. You must have some Jews in there, eh?'

'As God is my witness! I'm just fixing the stove.'

He came home in a temper, banging his fist on the table. 'Get the hell out of here! I didn't live through three years of this war safe and sound in order to go to a concentration camp on your account.'

'Marcin,' his wife tried to calm him. 'The walls have ears.'

'Let the neighbours hear once and for all,' he thundered.

'All right, I'm going,' said Viktor.

'Now?' Husband and wife gave a start.

'Only where to?' Viktor wondered out loud.

Majewski fell back with a groan.

'You know what,' Viktor suggested, 'let me give you some money to buy a big closet with. You can bring it in parts and assemble it here. I'll stay in it all day long.'

'Whatever you say,' Majewski shook his head. 'It looks like you're just our bad luck.'

'The man will be the ruin of us,' sobbed his wife.

'There, there, don't you cry, woman,' Marcin tried to console her. 'You'd better go and pawn something, the cabbage in the bin is all rotted. Never mind, we'll get ourselves a closet after the war.'

13

Browned to perfection, the meatballs gave off a bright wisp of smoke. Golden gravy dripped into the pocket of the mashed potatoes, turning them a yellowish colour.

'Where's the spoon?' Yurik whispered in his sleep, groping for it over his brother's face.

Kazik woke up. 'Move your hand.'

'What happened?'

'You're scratching my face.'

Yurik awoke. 'I must have been dreaming. She said that if I used the spoon . . .' He didn't go on. Instead he jumped out of bed, feeling around his underpants. 'The coins!'

Kazik sat up. 'Are they gone?'

'I can't see them,' Yurik whispered.

'Do you have any matches?'

'Yes, but the candle's burned down.'

'Go and swipe one from the kitchen.'

Kazik slipped out of bed and started up the stairs from the cellar. A floorboard creaked under his feet. He stopped and listened tensely.

'Maybe you can find some bread there too,' Yurik whispered from the door.

'Not a chance, she hides it in her room.'

Kazik came back with a candle and they lit it. The flame cast its light on the red brick walls and the compacted ground at their feet. Yurik threw the sacks off the straw matting and they began to search for the coins. A fraternity of fattened bedbugs scurried from under their hands. Kazik licked a finger and grabbed one of them.

'I've got it!'

'Give it here, I'll roast it in the candle.'

Yurik pressed the insect into the melted tallow, perfectly preserving its shape.

'Another one!'

They spent two hours searching through the straw for the twenty-dollar gold pieces.

'I have them!' Yurik cried triumphantly. He pulled a cloth bag from the straw. Kazik put the sacks back on the matting and they lay down to sleep again.

'Where's that safety pin you had?' asked Yurik. 'Let me have it. I'll pin the bag up tight.'

Kazik held up the stump of the candle. 'Look,' he said excitedly.

The bedbugs, which they had continued hunting all through the search for the coins, now formed a solid mass in the tallow. Yurik inspected the artifact. 'We'll keep it,' he decided. He blew out the candle and curled up under his blanket.

'Stop scratching.'

'It itches.'

'Aunt Ella said that if you scratch, the sores just get worse. Stop scratching.'

'As though you didn't scratch yourself,' said Kazik.

Dawn broke through the barred window high in the cellar wall.

'Kazik, come quick, it's a real fight!'

Kazik jumped down from the table and ran to the door. He looked through the keyhole while Yurik pressed his ear to the door. 'He's taking out the shovel from the tool box,' he whispered dramatically. 'Wow!'

There was running in the kitchen. 'I'll kill him!' shouted the old man.

'Pa, that's enough,' Yurik heard.

'That must be the younger one,' said Kazik from his place at the keyhole. 'He's breaking it up.'

'And Zigmund?' Yurik asked in a whisper.

'He's sitting there. I can only see his feet.'

'He's broken my hand,' Martha groaned. 'God will punish you.'

'He's put the shovel back,' Kazik said, disappointed.

'You no good, whoremongering bastard!' Yurik heard the old man shout, banging on the table. 'The damned sissy hasn't done anything for thirty-two years except go dancing and promenading at night. Why don't you get yourself a job and get married, you scum!'

'He's just thrown his cigarette on the floor,' whispered Kazik.

'Who?'

'Zigmund, who else?'

'What's his brother doing?'

'Eating. Zigmund's getting up.'

'You'd think both of you were born with silver spoons in your mouths,' said Zigmund, stamping out his cigarette with his heel. 'Who the hell brings you all the things from the ghetto? Who found you those two little kikes to pay you good money for rotting away in your cellar? That paragon of virtue over there?' He pointed scornfully at his brother. 'All he's good for is running a still in the cellar. Big hero! Him and that broad of his he's always with. Tfu!' He spat on the floor. 'It's me you're all living off!' he shouted. 'Hey, you eating over there, I'm talking about you too! He's a regular saint, he is. Maybe it's that pay-cheque of yours that you bring home from the factory that keeps us going? It's not even enough to buy bread with.'

'Shut up,' growled the old man. 'The factory's none of your business. And keep your hands off your mother.' He lost his temper again. 'You won't get out of here alive if I ever catch you doing that again! And you better not forget it.'

'Be quiet,' Martha tried to calm them. 'I can hear the neighbours coming. Sit down and eat.'

'Come in, come in and sit down,' she said to the woman at the door.

Yurik heard a bench being dragged across the floor.

'God bless. Why are you holding your hand like that, Martha?'

'I tripped in the dark and gave it a bang. Here, here's another stool. Sit yourselves down.'

'Is the door locked?' whispered Yurik.

'Yes.'

'Don't move.'

'I'm not moving.'

'Don't shake your leg like that.'

'No one can hear it.'

'I told you to stop.'

Kazik kept silently shaking his leg.

'As soon as they're gone you're going to get it,' Yurik threatened.

Kazik kept it up. Yurik tried pretending that it was none of his concern, but it wasn't any use. 'Stop it, you fool, they'll hear you.'

Kazik finally stopped. 'Give me the potty,' he said.

'Not now. Hold it in.'

'I can't.'

'You always have to go.'

'Are you going to give it to me?'

'No.'

Kazik tiptoed to the footstool and took out the potty from under it.

'Don't make so much noise,' Yurik whispered in despair. 'Go against the sides.'

'You know what?'

'What?'

'She caught me today with my hand in the soup.'

'What did you say?'

'That I was trying to get a fly out.'

'What did she say?'

'Nothing.'

'They're leaving.'

They could hear the visitors leaving the kitchen. Martha put the leftovers from the table on two plates and took them down to the cellar.

'Here, eat. Tomorrow I'll bring you a rabbit to play with.'

'A real live one?'

'How else would you play with it? Bring up the plates when you're finished.'

Martha returned to the kitchen. Her husband and eldest

son went to bed, while her youngest remained at the table, reading a newspaper.

'I brought you a bottle of oil, Mama.'

'That's just what I needed,' she said happily. 'I was almost out of it. How's your liquor doing? I just pray that no one tells on you, God forbid.'

'Don't you worry, Mama.'

'Did you ask Pani Kosopolska to bring medicine for the children?'

'Yes, she promised she would.'

'There's something about that woman I don't like,' Martha declared. 'She runs around too much. And the medicine must be brought. They're covered with running sores.'

'What's the matter with them?'

Martha shrugged. 'Some Jewish sickness.'

Yurik brought up the plates.

'Put them on the table,' she said. 'Are you still hungry?'

'Yes,' he said, embarrassed.

'You know, when you're hungry it means that your stomach is empty. You can always fill it with a little fresh water. Take a clean glass and drink up. What did your father do?'

'My father is a doctor.'

'Doctor Kosopolski? Not everyone can be a doctor, yet there's fate for you : now you're all on the run from one place to another. There's never any telling what God will do next. A man can be rich and get a cancer that all his money can't cure. That's how it is.'

Martha put out the light in the kitchen and went to her room.

'Martha? I'm going for a walk around the house.'

Her husband took the lantern and stepped out. Martha took the picture of their dead daughter down from its hook on the wall and looked at it.

'Matchei,' she said in a whisper to her husband when he returned. 'What would you say to taking in Marilka the orphan and bringing her up in our house?'

He thought it over. 'Take her in, if it'll please you. She can help you around the house.'

'I'll have a talk with the priest,' Martha decided.

'It looks like the sow will give birth tomorrow,' he said. 'Have you had this month's payment for the little Jews yet?'

'She was a day late with it.'

'We'll forgive her for that.' He undressed and got into bed.

'I don't like the looks of her, that Kosopolska.'

'Enough.' He turned his back to her and curled up in his blanket.

Martha kneeled before the icon of the Virgin and immersed herself in prayer.

The hands of the saints and the martyrs in the pictures on the walls now seemed to be made out of wax; a halo of light shone round their heads in the darkness. They looked down on her pale-faced and red-lipped, and in their expressionless eyes a hidden smile seemed to play.

The boys awoke one morning to find a new tenant in their room. His name was Doctor Rubin. He offered them bread and jam.

'No thanks, Pan Doctor.'

'You sure you don't want any, boys?'

'No thanks.'

Doctor Rubin put the bread and the jar of jam back into the drawer of the desk and left the cellar.

'Stand by the door,' ordered Yurik. 'Is he coming back?'

'No.'

Yurik opened the drawer and hurriedly cut two slices of bread. He held out the open jar to his brother. 'Quick, take a fingerful, someone's coming.'

It was only Doctor Rubin returning to the kitchen to talk to Martha. 'There were one hundred and forty of us in the family, and now there are only six of us left. And the war isn't even over yet. What a catastrophe! Just look at those two boys. . . .'

'I know, Pan Doctor,' said Martha. 'These are bad times. To think that I would one day have to hide you in my house!'

'She used to be their maid,' whispered Yurik.

'How do you know?'

'He told me.'

'And you have no idea who might have informed on me?' asked Doctor Rubin.

Martha shrugged. 'Maybe Piotrokowska. She has it in for Jews. She must have gone to collect the reward money.'

'Just a few more days, Martha,' he promised.

'Really,' she apologized, 'I wasn't thinking of that at all. But three Jews in one house . . . my husband is afraid.'

They were silent for a while. 'I think someone's coming. Hurry up and get under the bed.'

Doctor Rubin ran down to the cellar instead and shut the door after him. Yurik turned his face to the wall while he swallowed his last bite of bread. Kazik hid his slice in his pocket.

'Someone's coming,' said Doctor Rubin. 'Try to behave quietly now.'

There was talking in the hallway and then Martha came down. 'There's a message for you,' she said.

The doctor took the envelope from her and opened it. He quickly scanned what was written in it. '*Mein Gott,*' he gasped, 'Stashek's got papers from Uruguay for us. They must be worth something, or he wouldn't have done it. Is the policeman still here?'

'Yes,' said Martha. 'He's waiting inside.'

'Martha, we're going to Uruguay!' he cried happily. 'It's far away in South America.' He put on his coat and his hat. 'Goodbye boys. Take care.'

'Goodbye Pan Doctor,' they chorused.

'At last we can do whatever we want down here again,' said Yurik when he had left.

'He forgot his bread,' announced Kazik, hurrying to open the desk drawer.

'Are you keeping count?'

'Yes.'

'Uncle Edek,' said Yurik. 'Our two uncles and aunts from Czestochow. Little Gutzo. Grandfather. Mama. Uncle Ignatz.'

'Uncle Ignatz doesn't count,' Kazik said. 'He was a soldier in the Red Army.'

'It makes no difference. As long as it was Germans. Keep counting. Yujo, Marisha . . . who else was in Czestochow?'

'I don't remember.'

'How many so far?'

Kazik counted on his fingers. 'Eleven,' he said.

'Now Papa's side. Aunt Anka and Uncle Sokol. Grandfather and Grandmother. Uncle Mundek for sure too, and Aunt Ella's husband, the pilot. And you remember, once an old lady came to see us and Mama said that she was some kind of distant aunt of ours? They must have got her too. How many does that make?'

'Seven.'

'Who else? Wait, don't you remember Uncle Sokol's red-headed sister and her husband and the two children? That's four more.'

'Eleven,' Kazik added. 'Altogether it makes twenty-two.'

'Yoasha's father and Uncle Vilek who married Stella.'

'Twenty-four.'

'Should we count Papa too?'

'No.'

'Then that's all. There are more than six of us left. But how could there have been one hundred and forty people in his family? He must have counted all his distant relatives. We don't even know who ours are.'

'Pani Martha?'

'Yes, Kazik.'

'Could you let me have some dough? We're baking bread for our dolls.'

'Did she give you any?' Yurik asked.

'Yes, lots.'

'Look, I'm writing the inside page in plain handwriting,' Yurik said. 'I don't have the patience to print.'

'Did they drown in the end?'

'Read it and see. There's still one more instalment to come.'

Yurik continued to work on issue number two of their newspaper with his tongue pointing out of his mouth. He had written the whole first page in capital letters. In the middle of it was a drawing of an old Polish coin captioned by the story title : 'The Adventures of an Ancient Coin.'

'Let me do something too,' Kazik asked.

'Print some money. Make each note worth ten crowns.'

'Should I just write the numbers?'

'Yes.'

Kazik took some slips of paper and began to write on them : 10, 10, 10, 10.

Yurik glanced up at him. 'It won't do you any good to steal. I've made a new watermark.'

'I wasn't stealing,' protested Kazik. 'Show me the watermark,' he asked.

Yurik searched through his pocket and took out a stamp made from cork. 'See the letters in the middle? That's B1, for First Bank. But if you break up the B, you can read it 131 too, like a number.'

'That's got a lucky thirteen in it,' said Kazik. 'Will you sell me another dress like your wife has?'

'No,' Yurik refused. 'The wife of the Commander of the Universe has to have a nicer dress than your wife.'

'But my wife is your sister-in-law.'

'That doesn't matter.'

'When are you going to make me a wife for Ironhand?'

'Tomorrow,' Yurik promised.

Kazik began to take out his entourage from under the bed and to inspect it one by one. 'I don't have any means of getting to the party,' he announced. 'My carriage is broken.'

'What about the black car?'

'The wheels fell off.'

'Give it to me, I'll glue them back on. But you'll have to pay me for it.'

Kazik groped in his hiding place in the wall and pulled out a few notes. 'How much?'

'A hundred crowns. And you owe me another five hundred for your wife's wardrobe.'

'Should we start the party?'

'All right, take out the bank. Let's begin.'

All the candles in the cardboard building were lit, throwing a yellowish light over the mirrors and old furniture and burnishing the display of arms on the tapestried walls of the bank. Silent servants flanked the steps and the walls of the great hall, waiting for a signal. The president's own guard of honour stood at attention along the avenue leading to the First Bank Castle, dressed in dashing uniforms with tricorns on their heads. Each soldier was unusually tall, except for Pan Wolodiowski, the internationally famous fencing master, who stood at the head of the guard.

The trumpeters sounded a fanfare, the presidential flag was run up the flagpole, and the guests of honour turned down the avenue. The officers of the guard of honour drew their swords and the soldiers presented arms. Yurik poured the chess pieces out of their box and arranged them behind the soldiers.

'These are the cheering masses,' he said. 'Long live Jan Grenadier Tarzan, Commander of the Universe!'

'Don't forget me,' Kazik reminded him.

'Long live Richard Grenadier, his brother!' Yurik added.

The president and his wife, accompanied by generals, entered the gates of the castle and mounted the broad steps leading up to the hall. Among the guests were General Captain Nemo, General Swircziewski, General Sikorski, General Gordon, General Kosciusko, General Admiral Nelson, General Poniatowski, and many others, all wearing medals of honour and full ceremonial dress.

Now Kazik entered with his wife and the generals of the Opposition, among them Ironhand, who had been promoted at a special roll call that morning. On his left marched General Robin Hood, his bow slung over his shoulder.

Chairs were brought to the long, sumptuously set table and all the officers sat down.

'We can pretend that they've already danced in another hall,' said Yurik.

'What did they dance?'

'A polonaise,' Yurik said. 'Like the one in my reader from school. I went first with my wife, and then all the generals danced in couples and then the rest of the guests. The orchestra played and we all promenaded around the hall.'

'Fine,' Kazik agreed.

Jan Grenadier Tarzan rose to his feet and proposed a toast to the Fatherland. All the guests rose too.

'Long live Poland!' thundered the two boys.

Jan Grenadier Tarzan turned his glass bottom up.

'Cannon!' ordered General Boehm. The one hundred and twenty cannon of the invincible First Bank roared their approval of the presidential toast.

'Long live the First Bank!' shouted Yurik, throwing his glass against the wall of the hall, where it shattered to pieces.

'Long live Tarzan!' shouted the guests, breaking their glasses too.

'Long live me!' cried Kazik in a mighty voice.

'You can't toast yourself. Let Ironhand do it.'

The banquet began. Kazik took out the dough and the two of them bolted it down. Yurik spread out the newspaper and read in a solemn voice : 'The First Bank Gazette, Issue Two, Warsaw, the Twelfth of June, Nineteen hundred and forty-three.'

Ella burst into the cellar. 'Boys, get dressed quick. You're going to Palestine.'

Yurik began to shiver, felt nauseous, and ran to the corner to puke.

A department of the German Foreign Office had decided to draw up a list of Jews holding foreign passports and to assemble them in one of the camps so that they might be exchanged for German nationals interned by the Allies. Most of these passport holders were no longer alive. The order was sent from Berlin to the Gestapo in Warsaw, which turned it over for execution to the Jewish Gestapo, as the Jewish collaborators with the Nazi occupiers were called. A first detachment of foreign nationals had already been assembled in the Hotel Royal in Warsaw, from where it was shipped, according to eye-witness reports, in a westerly direction rather than eastward or south-eastward to the death camps. Furthermore, it was said that the entire detachment had been sent in the second- and third-class compartments of the regular train service. A second detachment was to be assembled in the Hotel Poland, whose lobby was quickly flooded by claimants to foreign citizenship, by Jews hiding on the Polish side desperate enough to grasp at any straw, and by the Jewish Gestapo itself. Whoever had the money paid staggering sums for Paraguayan, Uruguayan, or some other distant country's papers, changed his name to that on the document, and wrote in the additional names of as many members of his family as he could. In some cases he really had a family; in others, out of the goodness of his heart or for a price, he agreed to adopt perfect strangers. Among the foreign nationalities for sale were some two hundred Palestinian ones, which were considered to be of lesser value than the others. These were bargained for by the poorer of the bidders, who were happy to get what they could.

Upon escaping from the factory Stella had spent several weeks with her sister. Eventually, though, she had been forced to leave under threat of disclosure, for one day the landlord, hoping that if Stella left in a hurry she would leave all her possessions behind, told her that the Gestapo was coming. The landlady's calculations proved correct.

Viktor Finkel, too, was unable to stay any longer with the Majewskis, and one day the two of them turned up at the Hotel Poland.

Anna had tried to argue Stella out of it. 'You're making a fatal mistake. It's just another trap. At least leave the boys here in Warsaw.'

'The boys will come with me,' said Stella, cutting short the debate.

Anna left the hotel.

Stella had enough money to buy two South American passports and two Palestinian ones. But Stella also had a mystical side to her. Sofia had once made her swear that she would never abandon the boys and would always stay with them. She decided to buy four Palestinian passports.

'You make me laugh,' said Viktor.

'I believe in what I believe in, and none of my beliefs have ever failed me.'

Viktor went to take care of the Palestinian papers. Stella ran into G. in one of the corridors of the hotel. She didn't even look at him as she walked by. He was on the Palestinian list too.

The Hotel Poland bustled with people. Everyone had his own story. Everyone called it something else, a miracle, or divine providence, or destiny, or blind chance. The day Viktor and Stella arrived in the hotel the cover rose from a manhole in the building's plumbing system and two filthy, wild-haired figures emerged.

'You're in the Hotel Poland,' they were told.

The two survivors of the ghetto revolt were added free-of-charge to somebody's South American family.

It was a summer day. Yurik and Kazik were blinded by the sunlight and made giddy by all the fresh air.

'Look!' Kazik said. 'A butterfly.'

But Yurik was anxiously watching a gang of boys who were quarrelling over something at the end of the street.

The boys travelled to Warsaw on a narrow-gauge train whose locomotive looked more like a toy than a real one. Once in the city they took a trolley-bus. 'I smell a Moyshe here,' said one of the passengers, and at that exact moment someone else shoved them aside and jumped from the speeding car. Two other men jumped after him.

Zigmund brought them as far as the hotel.

'Good God!' cried Stella when she saw them. 'Sit down, I'll bring you something to eat.'

They sat and she brought meat, bread and butter, spreading piece after piece for them, silently watching the loaf of bread as it rapidly disappeared.

'It's a royal banquet,' Yurik enthused, biting into a cold chicken sandwich.

Kazik ate steadily though more slowly.

'What did the doctor say?' asked Viktor.

'He said they have a bad case of scabies. They also have sores that come from an unbalanced metabolism. He said they'll get better only slowly.'

'If we have a medical inspection at the border they'll never let us through.'

'Stop being such a prophet of doom,' Stella said. 'Are you finished, boys? Rest a while and then we'll go to the barber.'

Viktor lowered his voice. 'What did you do with the diamonds?'

'They're here.' She pointed to the hard-boiled eggs. 'We'll add the gold coins that the boys brought to the sandwiches.'

'When is Ella coming with the suitcases?' he asked.

'Tomorrow. That silly goose has gone and fallen in love with G. She even brought his suitcases today.'

'That's all we needed,' said Viktor. He went out into the corridor to see if there was any news.

In the morning the hotel's doors were shut and the foreign passport holders were taken to the railway station. Anna and Ella followed in the street, watching furtively to see what happened. The passengers were put into second- and third-class compartments and the entire detachment of two thousand five hundred people was sent westward, away from death.

Two years later only three hundred and fifty of them would still be alive, among them the two hundred on the Palestinian list.

A third shipment of foreign nationals was to leave the Hotel Poland too. This one, however, like that of other Jews, travelled east by south-east.

I took out my handkerchief and waved at the departing train, unable to make myself heard.

'We're moving,' Yurik said happily. 'Do you hear the wheels? They sound just like real ones.'

Kazik stuck his head out the window and looked excitedly at the panting locomotive.

'Kazhiula, keep your head inside the carriage,' Stella told him.

Poznan. Berlin.

'This is where Hitler lives,' Kazik said.

Then Rathenow, Stendal. It was already the next afternoon. Fields dotted with white farmhouses, their roofs made of red tile, stretched into the distance.

'It doesn't look like Poland,' said Kazik.

'It's a more civilized country here,' explained Viktor.

'Yes,' Stella repeated, 'civilized. You seem to have forgotten what year we're living in.'

Towards evening they reached a station near Hanover called Bergen. Soldiers politely helped the women and children into waiting trucks and handed up their possessions after them. The convoy took them to a camp of wooden cabins called Belsen.

Bergen-Belsen.

14

Stella called for the camp doctor. The two boys lay next to each other on their mattresses, smelling strongly of ointment.

Yurik turned to his brother. 'Did you really faint?'

'Yes.'

'What's it like?'

'Your eyes get dark and you fall. Aunt Stella caught me.'

'What did the doctor say?'

'That the ointment was too strong.'

From the other end of the cabin came the voices of two women and a man.

'I wouldn't have fainted,' said Yurik.

'You would.'

'I'm taking the chairs back right this minute, Pani!'

'I dare you to try.'

'But Pani Stella,' the calmer voice of the husband tried to persuade her, 'the chairs are ours.'

'Pan Roza,' said Stella, 'the boys are sick and I need chairs.'

'You stole them and you'll return them!' shrilled his wife.

The three of them stood by the two boys.

'All right then, take your chairs. But remember that I asked you not to. Come, Yurik, I'll put the ointment on you first today. I can see that the pus is getting less.'

Pan Roza nudged his wife with an elbow. 'Come on, Fanya, let's go,' he whispered.

'You haven't heard the last of this, Pani,' the woman shouted as her husband dragged her away.

'What a pair of idiots,' laughed Stella. 'Come on Yurik, let's go outside. Well, why don't you take your clothes off? That's right, all of them. Your underpants too.'

'I'm embarrassed,' Yurik said.

'What are you embarrassed about? You've nothing to worry about. Take them off right now. Nobody's looking at you and nobody could care less.'

'I don't want to.'

Stella put down the tube in her hand and undressed him forcibly. 'You stubborn fool! Come here.'

Three clear and sunny summer months went by. The food and fresh air had their effect and the boys regained their health. The weather was crisp and the skies were blue. The camp was composed of cabins surrounded by barbed wire, beyond which were more camps of cabins surrounded by more barbed wire, and more camps and more cabins as far as the eye could see. Sentries patrolled between the wire fences, sometimes with dogs, made the rounds of the cabins, and stood in watchtowers with machine guns and searchlights at night. But none of this belongs to our story; neither the cabins of the shaven-haired men nor those of the women; neither the cabins of those condemned to die from hunger and overwork nor those of prisoners consigned to experiments called 'medical'. Our story concerns just two

178

boys who came to this place by sheer chance and the cabin in which they lived – a longish hut painted green on the outside with a black tarpaper roof and a wooden plank floor, the trodden earth outside admitting only a few sparse weeds to the sunlight. Its toys were a stamp album, a wooden man the height of a finger, and many lead soldiers.

'Kazik, put him up front so he can salute. Forward march!'

Back and forth. Tanks and artillery headed for the front, airplanes cut through the air. The boys guided their soldiers around the room and mourned their heroes when they fell – but what else was there to play at if not war? They made themselves new heroes, cut out flags and insignias, fought for the fatherland, and shouted: Long live! Or: Freedom! Or: Charge! When they had finished they put their soldiers away in a box, while the tanks and artillery rumbled on through the world. At night there were stars in the sky, in summer clouds of rain and in winter clouds of snow.

At the end of that first summer a high official arrived from Berlin, a man of many years' service in the SS.

Some two thousand seven hundred people were sent eastward to be incinerated at Auschwitz. Among them were ex-members of the Jewish Gestapo and survivors of the ghetto revolt. Parents who had bought their children better passports than themselves now said goodbye to them.

The eight hundred or nine hundred survivors were moved to a smaller camp.

'Go and tell your uncle that you're sorry,' Stella demanded. 'Just because you call him uncle doesn't mean you can be impertinent to him. Go and apologize immediately!'

Yurik went. He found Viktor Finkel sitting on his bed in the men's cabin with his arms around Kazik. 'You know what, Uncle Viktor?' whispered Kazik. 'When we're freed and I'm big I'll get awfully rich and I'll buy you one of those chairs you can rock in. You'll sit and rock on our front porch and play with my children.'

'You're a good boy,' Viktor said emotionally. Yurik approached them. Viktor cleaned his glasses and put them back on again.

Yurik stood there.

'Will you never call me that word again?' asked Viktor.

Yurik didn't answer. 'You know what, Uncle Viktor,' he said, 'if you give me your socks I'll mend them for you.'

'Yurik, go and queue up, the soup pots are coming around.'

'Let Kazik go.'

'Go right this minute, do you hear me? Kazik went this morning.'

'I'll go twice the next time.'

'All right,' Stella consented. 'But don't forget.'

Yurik was writing a poem. He had written eighteen of them already and had even declaimed one out loud when the children put on a show for the camp. It hadn't been one of his best poems. There were better ones, but those he wouldn't show to anyone.

He wrote :

> I stand at the parting of ways
> Unsure where to turn though alive.
> Though their path leads over fresh graves
> The thieves, cheats and murderers thrive.

Another poem went :

> . . . For millions of years without stop
> They march down life's road without knowing
> They're not even the tiniest drop
> In a river that never stops flowing.

It wasn't so good to use the word 'stop' twice in the same stanza, he thought.

'Yurik, come and eat.'

He swung his legs over the side of the bed and slipped down.

Stella tasted the soup. 'You boys can eat mine. This soup isn't good for me. I'll take a piece of bread. Viktor, leave that bowl alone. You've already eaten.'

'Yes,' said Viktor, still swallowing the soup.

Stella was silent.

'Aunt Stella said not to eat her soup,' Yurik said.

'Don't butt in,' she scolded him. 'How many times do I have to tell you that?'

'But he's still eating!'

'Be quiet!' She opened the suitcase of food and took out a homemade scale.

'Here's a hundred grams of bread, Yurik. Give them to your teacher for last week. Have you done your homework?'

'Yes,' Yurik said. He took a piece of broken board covered with pencil writing from under his mattress. Stella cut two more slices and gave them to the boys. 'Here, this is for your milk.'

Yurik began to eat his piece right away. 'Kazik, aren't you going to eat yours now?'

'No, I'm leaving it for my milk.'

'He's weaving it for his wilk,' Yurik mimicked him.

'Leave him alone,' Stella said. 'If you want to eat your

bread now, go ahead and eat it.'

'I already have,' he said.

Kazik laid his slice of bread on the suitcase cover and cut it into cubes with a knife. 'I've got fourteen,' he counted, sweeping them into his cup with his hand. He shook the cup noisily.

'I've got fourteen . . .' said Yurik. Kazik kept shaking the cup.

'What are you waiting for?' Stella prodded them. 'Take your cups and go.'

Stella had lied about the boys' age, making them two years younger than they were, to get them a bigger milk ration.

'Kazik, when were you born?'

'In nineteen thirty-five.'

'And you?'

'In nineteen thirty-three.'

'Don't forget it. And your name is Kosowolski again, not Kosopolski. What's my name?'

'Stella Finkel,' said Kazik.

An American bomber flew low overhead, chased by two German fighter planes. Bullets splattered over the roof and the ground. A few people took cover in the ditch near the cabins. Kazik tripped on the doorstep with his cup that held fourteen cubes of bread and a dozen children and adults fell on top of him.

The fighters whistled sharply back in stubborn pursuit of the bomber. On their third pass overhead the American plane caught fire and fell, leaving behind it a white trail of smoke and a slowly descending parachute that bobbed on the wind. Four helmeted motorcyclists roared down the road by the camp. Kazik was already on his feet and back at the front of the milk queue. Yurik's cup was empty when he returned to the cabin.

'Did you hurt yourself when you fell, Kazhiula?' Stella asked anxiously. 'Did all your bread spill?'

'Some chance of that,' said Yurik.

Kazik sat on the bed and began to eat. Yurik looked over his shoulder.

'What a pig!' he said, staring at the fourteen cubes of bread as they floated in the milk.

Kazik smacked his lips. Stella burst out laughing.

'Are those two Finkel's kids?'

'Yes, over there.'

'Tfu!' spat the first man. 'I can't stomach him.'

'A miserable speculator.'

'His wife's not the finest character either.'

'Come on now, she isn't that bad.'

'I must admit that she goes all out for her children.'

'He got a good beating yesterday.'

'Really? What a shame I wasn't there to enjoy it.'

Yurik had also seen Uncle Viktor being hit. He ran to hide behind the cabin and then went to tell Stella.

'You idiot!' she shouted. 'Why didn't you come to tell me right away? I'd have given them a lesson they wouldn't forget for the rest of their lives.'

Stella considered for a moment. The camp representative was fond of Yurik. He always came to shake his hand whenever he recited anything. 'Go to Pan Dienstein and tell him that your aunt would be most grateful to him if he could put in a good word for Uncle Viktor.'

Yurik didn't answer.

'Did you understand what I said? He likes you very much.'

Yurik thought of Pan Witkowski in Schultz's factory.

'Well, what are you waiting for?'

Yurik knocked on his door.

Pan Dienstein stood by the window with his hands in his pockets. 'What's the matter, young man?' he asked with concern, seeing Yurik's pale face and his spastically contracted right hand.

Yurik got hold of himself and flexed his hand with great effort. 'My aunt said she would be grateful if you'd stop them from hitting Uncle Viktor.'

Pan Dienstein laughed. 'All right, young man, all right. Run along now and don't worry.'

Yurik's birthday came in winter. Before the war it had always been a great event in his life. As soon as Christmas was over he would start counting the days until February, and then until the twenty-fourth of the month. In the morning he would awake without opening his eyes and slowly grope along the tabletop to find his presents. All day long his uncles, aunts and cousins would come with more gifts.

'This is from Aunt Stella and myself,' said Viktor Finkel, handing him a long object. 'It's an adjustable pencil that writes in five colours. Here, let me show you.' He took the present back from the boy.

'I'll work it out myself,' said Yurik.

'Many happy returns of the day,' Stella congratulated him. 'May you live to be a hundred and twenty.'

'One hundred will be enough,' said Viktor.

'Eat up,' she said.

Viktor, Kazik and Yurik reached out for a slice of the decorated bread that lay on top of the suitcase.

'You have a piece too,' said Viktor with his mouth full.

'It isn't for me,' answered Stella. 'I'll drink Yurik's milk.'

It was snowing outside. A few wan rays of light fell

through the fabulously frost-etched windows onto the long rows of bunks that lined the walls. People wrapped their blankets tighter around them and waited.

15

The second summer another group was sent eastward from the camp. It happened on a Tuesday, and the following Tuesday yet another group was sent. A third shipment was assembled too, but for some reason an order came through to detain it and its members were interned in a small camp of their own. Some three hundred or three hundred and fifty of the foreign passport holders were left. From now on starvation would shrink their numbers even more.

The bunks in their new cabin were triple-deckered and stood one against another. The exchange rates for bread and cigarettes had soared. Those for gold and clothing had fallen.

The Allies had landed on the shores of France and the German retreat from Russia had begun.

'This will be our boat,' said Yurik, drawing it on the ground. 'We'll dig a seat and play at whaling. Go and find some boards for oars,' he told Kazik. 'And one sharp one for a harpoon.'

The equipment was assembled and the boat hoisted sail. A fierce storm blew up.

'The waves are as high as a house,' Yurik cried enthusiastically. 'They're like skyscrapers. The boat is pitching up and down.'

'The mast has snapped!' Kazik cried.

'Hold onto the sail!' shouted Yurik. 'We'll need it to collect rainwater because all our food's been swept overboard.'

Kazik jumped from the boat and ran after the large sheet of paper. He made his way back with difficulty and clung to the gunwales of the boat. 'I nearly drowned,' he panted.

Yurik leaned the other way to keep the boat balanced while Kazik climbed in. 'Grab onto this cable! The storm's getting worse.'

'I can't hear you over the wind,' whispered Kazik.

'Tie yourself to the mast!' Yurik screamed. 'I'll tie myself to the rudder. Maybe we can ride it out.'

For a day and a night and another day they fought the furies of nature.

'I think the storm must have died down by now,' Kazik declared. 'Let's start hunting for whales.' He stood at the edge of the boat. 'I'm throwing them some breadcrumbs, maybe they'll come. Whaa-aales! Pss-pss-pss-pss-pss!'

'What a simpleton!' said Yurik pityingly. 'You think that a whale's like a pussycat?'

Yurik and Kazik stood outside the cabin trapping flies against the green wall, which was warm from the heat of the sun. Kazik carried a matchbox.

'I've got one! Open up.'

Kazik carefully pushed out the drawer of the box, keeping a finger over the narrow opening. Yurik held the fly by its wings and slipped it inside. Just then another fly managed to slip out. It stood on Kazik's finger and tried to straighten its wings.

'Let it go,' Yurik said. 'As it got out it may as well go free.'

Kazik held the box to his ear. 'We've got enough,' he said, listening to the buzzing.

They took a bowl, filled it with water, and floated three toothpicks tied together with thread. Yurik added a mast. A few matches served as lifeboats. They cut the flies' wings off and put them on the deck to be sailors.

'They're walking.'

'Two are on the mast.'

'One's jumped overboard! He's doing the crawl.'

Yurik began to sing :

> The fly's in the soup, the snake's in the grass
> Hitler is up the Polish man's arse.

'It'll drown.'

'No it won't.'

Kazik stirred the water with both hands. 'Waves!'

The boat capsized. The lifeboats floated on the water and several of the sailors grabbed onto them. Others crawled onto the overturned boat while still others struck out desperately for shore. Yurik watched them for a while, then picked up the lifeboats and threw them away.

'What are you doing?' Kazik complained.

'It's boring.'

'So are you. You never want to play anything any more.'

Kazik turned over the bowl of water. Wingless flies crawled around inside it, barely able to drag their own stickily wet bodies.

Yurik spent the second winter in bed.

'You're going to rot away. Get up and wash.'

'I don't want to.'

Viktor muttered something from the bunk beneath him. Yurik turned his face to the wall. There was a tap there.

A whole row of them. Sweet, warm milk flowed from one of them, honey from a second, meat and potatoes from a third. He only had to press a button for it all to vanish in the wall; another push and it all reappeared. He wouldn't give Uncle Viktor even a drop.

'Get down from there and empty out your night bottles,' Viktor shouted. 'Do you think I'm going to be your servant? It wouldn't hurt you if you went and helped your aunt to do the washing. She's too good for you. If I were her I'd teach you a proper lesson.'

Go to hell, Yurik thought, those smelly underpants are your own. But he didn't say anything. He got out of bed and went to the shower.

Stella stood by a wooden table scrubbing their underwear with frozen hands.

'Have you come to help? Here, rinse these under the tap. Hurry up, I'd like to finish before roll call.'

Yurik rinsed the wash, sticking his fingers into his mouth to warm them. It was snowing outside. Once more the window panes were covered with flowers, butterflies, even an occasional mountain or pond of ice. A bit of light filtered through among the high, crowded bunks on which people were huddled in blankets, still waiting.

'If only we can hold out until spring,' Stella said. 'Just until spring.'

16

Spring came. Five men wearing faded coats and wooden clogs on their feet stood by the barbed-wire fence. A few feet away stood three similar-looking men, whilst another stood off by himself. The yard was full of puddles and mud. The men leaning on the fence looked to see what was going on in the kitchen or gazed out at the traffic on the road. Yurik came towards them across the yard. He neared the fence, dragging his clogs that were too large for his feet and occasionally skating on them over the mud. He stood between the three men and the one man, pressing hard against the fence with his face stuck through the wires.

The German cook, a fat soldier with an apron, appeared in the kitchen doorway. He stuck his hands into his pockets and leaned against the door.

'He's warm enough, he doesn't need a coat,' said one of the three men.

'Of course, what do you think? He's got it good!' said the second.

'He must have greased someone's palm with a bundle to get posted here,' said the third.

An old soldier was limping towards them along the road. The cook returned to the kitchen.

'Hey, Grandpa, how's Grandma?' shouted one of the group of five. The other men burst out laughing. The soldier, who had now reached the fence, shook a fist at them.

'Still, verfluchter Jude!'

'His kind don't shoot,' someone said. 'They were brought up in the old school.'

'Look at his uniform. It must be First World War surplus.'

'Where's your uncle?' one of the men asked Yurik.

'In the cabin.'

Two more soldiers approached from the left, looking like the first. One was tall and thin; the other, elderly too but short, hopped by his side.

'Your rifle's taller than you are, watch out you don't trip over it!'

The short soldier opened his mouth to answer. His comrade dragged him along, regarding the men at the fence with indifference as he strode erectly by, proud to be serving his country.

A wagon drawn by a pair of horses came by in the opposite direction. The wagoner walked alongside it with his hat pulled over his head, holding the reins in his hand. The hands and feet of corpses stuck out from under the canvas top. A boy's shaven head kept banging slackly against the back of the wagon.

'Clubbed,' the first of the three men standing next to Yurik said quietly.

'Damn it,' said the second, 'if only this damned war would stop.'

'Big deal if it does,' said the third. 'You think that just because it stops the world's going to turn inside-out? That's what I thought after the last war.'

A gang of prisoners came down the road in single file, each pushing a wheelbarrow piled high with earth. They trudged slowly, heads down, the corners of their striped shirts flapping in the wind. The wheelbarrows creaked on the road. Two guards tried to urge the prisoners on, brandishing clubs.

'*Vite, vite!*' one shouted in French.

The other shouted in Polish. '*Predko, predko!*'

A soldier with a gun and a helmet brought up the rear.

For a while the road was deserted. Then a female member of the SS, a blonde, came along with a quick, sprightly step.

'Shhh,' said one of the three men. 'That one's already killed a Dutchman.'

'The whore,' said another. 'I'd like to get my hands on a blonde cunt like that.'

'Did you hear about Helenka?' asked the third. 'She was

standing here yesterday and saw her mother among the prisoners on the road.'

'You're kidding!'

'It's a miracle from heaven,' said the first. 'Maybe they'll find each other again after the war.'

'They have a Ukranian kapo,' said the third. 'She beats them like a butcher. They were specially trained for that.' He turned up the collar of his coat. 'It's cold,' he said. He broke away from the fence and turned to go.

The two other men followed him. The group of five had already broken up, leaving only Yurik and the man standing by himself still leaning against the barbed wire, silently looking out.

Allied war planes flew over Bergen-Belsen all the next day. They passed slowly, at high altitude, wave after wave, glinting in the sun. They looked like tiny white birds flying in formation.

Yurik lay out of doors on a wooden bench and tried to count them. All of them.

There were fighter escorts and heavy bombers. Then came even heavier ones. He could feel the weight of their bomb loads in the throb of their motors. All day long they passed overhead, their monotonous drone unceasing above the camps.

They're heading for Hamburg, he thought, or perhaps for Berlin.

The soldier escorting them opened the gate and counted them off in threes.

'Yurik, watch the towels and the soap. Viktor, make sure the boys wash themselves well.'

'March,' ordered the soldier.

They tramped down the road. Some Russian prisoners of

war were still in the shower. Kazik left the line and went over to the wall to read the inscriptions carved in the plaster. *Rosenfeld Tarnow*, he read, and beneath it in pencil: *Krause Finkel and her daughter.*

'Uncle Viktor, perhaps it's a relative of yours?'

Viktor came over. 'Where?' he asked. 'What?'

'Here,' Kazik showed him.

'Does anyone have a pencil?' Viktor shouted. 'I've found my sister! Kazhiula, you darling.' He hugged the boy. 'A pencil, quick!' He waited for the soldier to turn his back and wrote next to the inscription: *Viktor Finkel, alive and well.*

Kazik dug an elbow into his brother's ribs. 'Did you see that?'

'You were just lucky,' said Yurik. 'If I'd gone over there I would have seen it too.'

The line began to enter and undress. A soldier counted the naked bodies. Viktor tripped on the wet planks and fell. Yurik turned his face to keep from laughing.

'You little ingrate, what are you so happy about?'

'I'm not happy,' he said. 'Kazik made me laugh.'

The soldier kept them moving. Hot, steamy water cascaded down. A second group was already waiting by the door.

Someone pushed against Viktor and the boys.

'Wait your turn,' shouted Viktor. 'There are already three people in here.'

'Boys aren't people.'

'Go over there. There are only two there.'

'Are you blind or something? Can't you see that there are four people everywhere but here?'

Viktor reached up to turn the nozzle towards himself and so did the stranger. Viktor grabbed it and hung on, his body dangling like a pendulum.

'Yurik,' said Kazik, 'give me the soap.'

'In a second. Maybe we should go somewhere else?'

'No, we can't leave Uncle Viktor.'

'To hell with Uncle Viktor,' whispered Yurik, and he added : 'You know, it gives me the creeps when he touches me with his wet, skinny arse.'

Yurik wrote a poem about Bergen-Belsen :

> Whole cities and countries have gone up in flame;
> But it's give us our soup and our bread and be gone!
> The world is in turmoil but we're still the same,
> And our life will go on, and go on, and go on.

He called the poem *Life*.

> I was sad, I was happy,
> I was good, I was bad,
> I rejoiced, I was mad,
> I was sorry and glad,
> And then over again
> I was happy and sad,
> Until I to the world
> A fond farewell bade.

He sat on his bunk, his head propped against the boards of the Grien brothers' bed, and composed a poem about the desert and a caravan that had vanished in its wastes :

> And after a year the wind blew through that land,
> And parted the dunes to reveal the bleached bodies dried;
> Through empty sockets the wakened skeletons eyed
> Themselves, and saw they were nothing but bones in
> the sand.

'What are you laughing at, Uncle Viktor?'

'I'm not laughing. I mean, I'm really crying. Your poem's really very sad.' Viktor burst out laughing again. 'It's a very good poem. Let me see the others you've written. Come on, let me see them.'

Yurik was offended and angrily hid his notebook. 'Never,' he said stubbornly.

'Move over, Uncle Viktor.'

Viktor pretended to be asleep. Yurik began to push him slowly across the bed.

'What are you trying to do, Yurik?'

'Move a little,' he whispered. 'I'm falling onto the neighbours.'

'Don't give me that. Lie quietly.'

'I'm really falling off the bed. And you've taken all the blanket.'

'Quiet. You'll wake your aunt.'

Yurik fell silent and listened to the bunk bed beneath them. Aunt Stella and Kazik were sleeping. The two Grien brothers turned over above them, making all three bed frames shake. Viktor began to snore. Yurik tried stealthily to capture part of the blanket. Viktor pulled it back.

'Let me have some of it, Uncle Viktor.'

Viktor was asleep.

Yurik gave it a jerk.

'You little runny-nosed snot! If you don't lie quietly like I told you I'll throw you out of bed.'

'I . . . I . . .' stuttered Yurik, his mouth full of un-uttered curses. You rotten stinking louse. You skinny son of a bitch. You every bad word I can think of. He grated his teeth. 'I . . .'

'You what?'

'Move over.' He was on the verge of tears.

'You have more room than I do, you nudnik. Give me your hand and I'll show you. All right, all right, I'll move a little.'

'You didn't move.'

'Of course I did,' Viktor said angrily.

'I can tell whether you moved or not, what are you telling me?'

'I tell you I moved. Shut up before you wake everyone.'

When he falls asleep again I'll push him right over the side, thought Yurik. He would sneak out of bed and eat all that was left of the Red Cross packages in the suitcase. There was still some Swiss cheese there. After the war he would run out onto the road and just keep going. . . .

Viktor slept. Yurik groped under the mattress and took out a cold baked potato. He put it in his mouth, trying to chew it as slowly as he could. When the potatoes had been distributed that day one had fallen to the ground and no one had seen it but him.

Someone nearby mumbled in his sleep, then let out a groan. A woman coughed. There was a scream. It was he himself shouting in his sleep: Kazik! Get out of that suitcase!

He awoke in the middle of the night and got up to inspect the row of bottles at the foot of the bed. He's filled them all up, he whispered bitterly to himself, and deliberately jabbed Viktor with his foot. Viktor slept on. Yurik crawled over him and made his way to the door through the narrow aisles between the bunks. It was a moonless night. He stood by the fence and urinated. The spotlight from the watchtower approached him, passed over him, then returned to him for a moment. Yurik tried to keep hitting the same barb of the wire with his pee. Then he looked up at the stars. He liked looking at them. It was like looking at a big secret.

Stella grabbed hold of him as he was getting back into bed.

'Where were you?'

Yurik didn't answer. Suddenly he threw his arms around her neck and burst out crying.

'There, there, don't cry.' She patted him on the head. 'The war will be over soon. You'll see, we'll find your father. Don't cry.'

Yurik began to write a new poem :

Mama . . .

17

'If it wasn't for the care packages your brother would have been gone from this world long ago, and don't think that you have unlimited powers either. It wouldn't do you any harm to lie down and rest. The boy's as pale as a sheet! I run around like crazy to get a proper diet for him and he burns the calories right up again.'

'I do lie down sometimes,' Yurik defended himself. 'Can I get dressed now?'

'All right, get dressed. But kill all the lice before you start throwing them down on me, all right?'

'All right. I found thirty-eight today.'

'I couldn't care less. What's going on outside? People are running.'

'We're leaving here tomorrow!' someone shouted from the door.

Yurik slipped quietly out of bed and went off to puke.

The order to pack up was given during one of the first

days of April. They had spent twenty-two months in Bergen-Belsen.

The next morning everyone shouldered his belongings as best as he could and headed for the railway station. Viktor carried two suitcases, Stella a suitcase and a knapsack, and Yurik two small carrying bags, his own and his brother's. Kazik felt dizzy and could barely walk.

'It's because he hasn't been out of bed for half a year,' Viktor said.

'Do you feel better now, Kazhiula?'

'Yes.'

'Here, drink a little water.'

The train was already waiting for them at the Belsen station. It was late at night when it finally pulled out with its load of two thousand five hundred people: Jews from Holland and from Hungary and from Greece; Jews with Spanish and Argentinian and Palestinian passports; and just plain ordinary Jews.

The train halted.

'Yurik, run!'

He jumped from the car and ran to the pile of beet fodder that stood at the edge of a nearby field. Just let me get back in time, he prayed. A soldier shot at him. He began to dash back. The train whistled and moved. Yurik got a foot on the step and swung himself back into the car.

'Put them here, under the bench. We'll cook up a soup.'

Stella took out a knife and began peeling and slicing the beets. 'You boys can help too,' she said.

The train stopped again.

Yurik jumped out with an empty tin can full of holes and filled it with kindling wood.

'Blow hard,' Stella said. 'It'll catch in a minute.'

Yurik lay on his stomach and blew hard.

The train moved.

The train stopped.

The train stood on a siding. They passed ruined stations, ruined houses, burned cattle-trucks turned upside-down.

'Viktor, don't drink that water. It's stagnant.'

'Right, right,' Viktor murmured, continuing to lap up the ditch water.

'You'll get dysentery,' Stella said angrily.

Kazik and Yurik lay down to fan the fire. Stella put on the beet soup. 'Come back to the car,' she said, 'and we'll eat it while it's hot.'

People were milling around by the front of the train.

'Perhaps they're giving out water by the locomotive? Yurik, take the can and go and see.'

Soldiers were throwing cans of tinned food from the flat-car on which the anti-aircraft and machine guns were mounted. Yurik managed to catch one. Kazik, who was following behind him, caught two. The soldiers were young. Some were blonde, smiling girls.

The train moved.

The train stopped.

Yurik counted the stations. On the afternoon of the fifth day the train stopped in a field by a forest. Planes circled overhead. The anti-aircraft gun opened fire. The airplanes didn't return it, though they kept circling low. Some passengers jumped from the cars and began to run for the forest. The soldiers shot at them.

'All we need now is for the Americans to start bombing,' Stella said.

The airplanes climbed and vanished. They were awakened that night by the approaching sounds of the front. Tracers lit the distant horizon and the thud of the cannon grew closer. Machine-gun fire could be heard too. Towards morning the train started up and began to move quickly. Yurik stood by the window, counting the mileposts.

'Twenty, twenty-one, twenty-two.'

'I don't know whether to laugh or cry,' Stella said.

Near Magdeburg the train stopped again. The locomotive and the flatcar of soldiers were unhooked from the train and rolled off. A few soldiers remained behind with them. Yurik went out for a walk. He saw a woman talking with a German soldier and stopped to listen. The soldier was holding a fish.

'*Komm, komm,*' he said to the woman, pointing with the fish to a path. The woman was bewildered. The soldier smiled. He turned around as though looking for someone and nearly ran into one of the Grien brothers.

'Hillel!' called the woman. 'He says there's fish, but I'm afraid to go with him by myself.'

Hillel went with her. Yurik trailed after them. The soldier brought them to a lake. Dead fish were floating on the water, their white bellies glinting in the sun.

'*Das kommt von einer Handgranate,*' explained the soldier. He picked up a branch, steered a juicy-looking fish to the shore, and handed it to the woman.

'*Auf wiedersehen,*' she said, and went off.

Yurik circled the lake, looking for a large fish, bending down to pick up the smaller ones near the shore as he did so. He collected them in his beret.

All the big ones were out in the middle of the water. Yurik prayed for a strong breeze. He waded into the water, wetting his shoes, and began to throw stones at a big fish. It started floating towards him. He kept aiming the stones carefully. He began to sing out loud, out of tune:

> *O Rosmarin, Rosmarin,*
> *La-la-la-la-la-la.*

Hillel laughed. '*Du kennst nisht zingen,*' he said in Yiddish.

Yurik shrugged. The fish was close enough to be pulled in with a branch. Hillel rolled up his coat and waded into the water with his boots on.

'What are you doing, Pan Hillel?'

Hillel reached out for the fish.

'Pan Hillel, it's mine. Can't you hear? Let go of it!'

Hillel slipped and fell into the water.

'*Mein Gott!* Save me, boy!'

Yurik was frightened. He held out the branch to him and Hillel grabbed hold of it and pulled himself ashore.

The fish was gone. He must have taken it, Yurik thought, watching the man disappear with something under his coat. Yurik picked up his beret and looked at the eyes of the dead fish inside it. You poor things, he said to them. Soon Aunt Stella will fry you. He folded the hat and went back to the train.

A unit of the American Ninth Army had reached the site of the train. The story went about that the first American soldier to reach them had been a Jew who had said: '*Yidden, sholom aleichem!*'

Kazik, Viktor and Stella went to pilfer food from a nearby German village. People hurried to hit the German soldiers. Yurik remained in the train to guard their possessions. He climbed on the bench and took down the suitcase of food. He began to eat: sausage, margarine, more jam, yesterday's soup – and threw it all up. Then he started all over again. He ate another half-loaf of bread with jam and margarine, and finished the sausage and yellow cheese. When an American jeep stopped outside to distribute food, he was already lying on the bench in a stupor. Stella and Kazik returned with eggs, an onion and a chicken. Kazik was all excited. 'You creep, you, do you know that we were the first to see the Americans? A jeep and tanks. Aunt Stella kissed a black man.'

'Don't touch me,' said Yurik.

Kazik went on telling him how Uncle Viktor had been taken straight to the hospital and that Roosevelt was dead.

Yurik didn't listen.

'You little fool!' Stella said, frightened. She shut the food suitcase and began rummaging through her medicines.

'Open your mouth.'

Yurik smelled it and squirmed with nausea.

'It's castor oil, idiot!' Stella fumed. 'Open your mouth or I'll shove the whole bottle down it. Do you want to have a blocked intestine? Open it!'

'I'd rather throw it all up.'

'All right then, throw up,' she agreed. She helped him out of the car and held his head.

'Are you finished?'

'Yes,' he groaned.

Kazik returned to the train. 'I've got chewing gum.'

Yurik said nothing.

'The Americans like to say *ho-kay.*'

'We're free!' shouted someone, dancing in front of the train.

Stella bent over a small fire, frying the fish. The oil bubbled and crackled. From time to time she raised her hand that held the tin fork and wiped the tears from her face with her sleeve.

18

A German officers' colony was evacuated for the refugees. It was composed of cottages, each with its own gardens and lawns, shady trees and arbours of roses. It was like a furnished Garden of Eden.

Friends of Stella's suggested that she stay with them, since she'd arrived too late to merit a house of her own. She came with the two boys. The three of them inspected the furniture.

'We'll bring two more beds in here,' Stella said. 'Try to clear a little space.'

'Should we take everything out?'

'No, just the bookcase and this sideboard.'

Yurik had a brainwave. 'Let's throw them out the window!'

Stella smiled. 'Fine,' she agreed. 'Kazhiula, go and get an axe. There's sure to be one in the kitchen.' She ran her fingers over the carvings on the fancy black buffet. 'It's an expensive old piece,' she said.

Kazik came back with an axe. 'Here,' he said.

'Put it down on the floor for a minute. The top part of this comes off. Have you got it? Let's go. Let's put it down for a second and make sure there's no one below. Watch out, I'm giving another push.'

They stuck their heads out the window. 'Death to the Germans!' shouted Kazik.

'All right,' said Stella. 'Now we'll need the axe, but let's use our brains. This thing must come apart naturally.'

They knocked off piece after piece and threw it outside to the cheers of the boys. People from the next house assembled below. An old man waved his cane at them. 'Barbarians!' he shouted. 'What are you doing? Barbarians!'

'Who are they?' asked Yurik.

'They're from Greece.' Stella leaned out the window. 'What right do you have to talk?' she shouted, 'How much did you suffer? How many of your family were killed? How many of your children were thrown out the window?

Get the hell out of here! Kazhiula, give me the chair.'
Kazik brought her the chair and she threw it down at them.
Yurik dragged a large pot with an agave in it from the
hall. 'Kazik,' he said, 'I need help.'
The two of them stood it on the window sill.
'Let me push,' Kazik begged.
'Together,' said Yurik.

Stella brought the children to the infirmary for a check-up.
Their temperature was normal.
'Now let's take yours,' the nurse said to Stella.
Stella smiled. 'There's nothing the matter with me.'
'It never hurts,' the nurse smiled back.
Stella had a high fever and was taken to the hospital.
The two boys returned home by themselves.

Yurik was keeping a diary. On the first page he had printed
in block letters : MAYBE.
'Why "maybe"?'
'Because we always said that maybe we'd survive.'
'Are you going to write about the whole war?'
'Yes,' Yurik said.
'That's a lot. I'm going.'
'Wait a minute. Look at this.'
Kazik bent over the notebook. 'What is it?'
'It's a chart of the war. The low points are when we
almost got killed.'
'And up here?'
'It's a secret.'
'Tell me.'
'What'll you give me for it?'
Kazik reflected. 'Two commands.'

'Up here is when we find Papa.'

'That's no secret,' Kazik said.

'You owe me two commands.'

'No I don't.'

'I'll beat you up,' Yurik threatened. Kazik ran off. Yurik stayed with his diary. Kazik went from house to house, looking for toys, searching through basements and attics. He already had a whole collection in his room: soldiers, cars, armoured troop carriers, tanks, ships, sailing boats, dice, and even a small locomotive that really worked.

Yurik lay on the floor organizing. 'From now on all our property will be in common,' he said.

'The five-coloured pencil too?' Kazik asked happily.

'No, birthday presents don't count.'

'All right,' Kazik agreed. 'Do you want to go and break stuff?'

'Where?'

'We found a factory with halls full of glass, and machines to make lenses. You can break there forever. All the kids go there.'

'I don't feel like it,' Yurik said.

'I'm going.'

'Fine, go. I'll get lunch and visit Aunt Stella.'

'Tell her I'll come and see her later,' Kazik said.

Yurik went to the hospital. On the street he saw two boys stop a young German riding on a bicycle.

'Get off!'

The German dismounted.

'Give us your trousers and shirt too.'

The German undressed.

Yurik asked if he could have a ride.

'Can you ride a bike?'

'Yes,' he said.

'All right, after we're finished.'

'I'll just take it for a spin and I'll go,' Yurik promised. 'I have to visit my mother in the hospital.'

He picked some roses by the hospital and brought them to Stella. Her bed was on the ground floor, and the boys liked to talk to her through the open window.

'I brought you some flowers.'

She smiled. 'However did you think of it? Thank you very much.' She talked very slowly, in a manner that was unlike herself. She opened her purse and showed him a packet of Polish cigarettes. 'Do you remember these?'

'Yes, I gave them to you once.'

'Now I can smoke them,' she said.

'Aunt Stella, you know, all the children are going to Palestine.'

'I know.'

'We want to go too.'

'Kazik too?'

'He hasn't said, but I want to.'

'You want to leave me here ill and go off? You really have no sense of gratitude,' she said bitterly. 'Well then, why don't you go?'

'Everyone's going,' Yurik apologized through the window.

The door of Stella's room opened and a doctor and nurse stepped inside. The nurse carried a large jar which she hung above Stella's head. Yurik shut his eyes. When he opened them again the needle that was attached to the jar by a rubber tube was already in her arm.

'Does it hurt?'

'Not very much.'

'I'll come again tomorrow. Kazik says he'll come later today.'

'Do you eat and wash yourselves occasionally?'

'Yes,' he said. 'Goodbye, Aunt Stella.'

She nodded goodbye. Two American soldiers were standing in front of the hospital, playing with a little ball which they threw and caught with a glove. Yurik stopped to watch them.

'Hey, boy, come here,' one of them called to him.

He felt embarrassed and ran off.

Viktor died. His soul departed from its decrepit hulk.

Listen here, Viktor tried to stop it, waving both his hands, wait just a second! I'm good for another thirty years. I've got rich relatives in South Africa. Hey, just a second!

But his soul continued on its upward flight, pale and transparent.

Wait a second! he called again desperately, searching through his pockets. If only I had a pair of socks here at least. Wait, I'll give you . . . you're bound for hell, you know, straight for hell.

It stopped.

I'm a basically kind fellow, he argued, and can still do a lot of people a lot of good. Come on back, he pleaded.

His soul wavered, the starry universe wheeling around it. What are you waiting for? asked the souls of two German soldiers as they flew by.

What are you waiting for? asked the soul of a young Australian rifleman.

What are you waiting for? asked the soul of a girl who had been killed in a bombardment a short while before. She might have been German, English or Japanese. Most souls look alike.

Are you coming back? Viktor asked.

A nurse entered the morgue and switched on the light. 'Here you are, doctor,' she said to the man behind her. 'Did you want to see number twelve?' She suddenly seized his hand in alarm.

'My God! One of them's moving.'
Viktor Finkel was returned to his room in the hospital.

Stella was completely recovered. Kazik opened the door for her. 'Aunt Stella's here!' he whooped. Yurik picked himself up off the floor. She stood in the doorway and looked questioningly inside.

'While everyone else has been collecting valuables and radio sets,' she said, 'I see you've been collecting toy soldiers. Not bad. We'll have a cosy future to look forward to now. If only it had occurred to you two little fools at least to stock up on canned food.'

'It's Kazik's fault,' said Yurik.

'Don't go blaming Kazik. You could have gone and done it yourself.'

'I'll go now,' Yurik said. 'I know where there's a chicken hanging in an attic, all pressed and dried like a violin.'

'Perhaps we can fiddle on it,' Stella said. 'Get all these toys out of here. I want to clean this junkyard up a little. And get yourselves out of here too.'

Kazik slid down the banister of the stairs. Yurik slid down after him. 'It's a pity she's back,' he said. 'That's the end of all our games.'

Yurik went swimming in the stream with the neighbours' daughter. He took a flute with him.

'Do you know how to play it?'

'No, I just make it up. I'll show you.'

They sat by the water in the shade of a branch. The girl picked flowers and began plaiting two wreaths, a yellow and a white one. 'Look,' she said.

'I see. Do you want to hear?'

'Yes.'

Yurik blew into the flute, opening and shutting the stops. He tried to make it sound as sad and wavering as he could.

'That's very nice,' she said.

The water lapped at their feet and reeds rustled in the breeze. A bird chirped.

'Should we go for a swim?' He took off his clothes and entered the water in his underpants. 'The water's warm, come on in!' he called.

She took off her skirt and stood there uncertainly with her blouse still on her shoulders.

'What's wrong?'

'Nothing.'

'Don't be silly, aren't we friends?'

She plucked up courage and undressed. Yurik stared at her as she slipped into the stream.

Afterwards they sunbathed on the grass.

'I can really swim a little,' he bragged.

'If you shut your eyes really tight,' she said to him, 'you can see all kinds of colours.'

'I always do that.'

'How many colours can you see?'

'Lots.'

'I like summer best,' he told her on their way back to town. They said goodbye at his house and Yurik raced up the stairs. He heard a door slam. An old, grey-haired woman dressed in black was coming down the stairs, hobbling on a cane. Yurik stepped politely aside to let her pass.

'Who is she?'

'Some filthy old German. She came to ask for her things. Some photograph of her sons. It's not enough for them that they killed millions of Jews. Just wait, I'm not done with her.' Stella ran to the garbage pail and took out the picture of Hitler.

'Hello!' she called out of the window. *'Hier ist Ihr Sohn.'*

The old lady made her way back to the house and Stella threw down the picture.

A jeep full of American soldiers with their arms round German girls passed down the road.

The war ended and the German surrender was signed. Magdeburg and its environs were assigned to the Soviet occupation zone. Stella went to get Viktor from the hospital. She saw him in the hall.

'Viktor, here,' she whispered. She gave him his clothes and he slipped them on over his robe.

'Come on, lean on me. There'll be transportation tomorrow morning to Magdeburg station.'

'Is anyone staying behind?'

'Just Pani Tomowicz,' said Stella. 'She wants to go back to Poland.'

They took a westbound train, fleeing from the Russians. They passed ruined industrial towns, bombed-out buildings, railway stations.

'What marvellous scenery,' Stella said pleasurably. She woke the two boys.

'Take a good look,' she urged them. 'You'll never see it again. There'll be plenty of time to sleep later.' Yurik opened his eyes and went to the window.

Kazik stayed glued to the window too. He kept looking for Germans. Whenever he saw one he made an executioner's sign at him.

'Who taught you that?'

'Everyone does it. Try it.'

Yurik grabbed his hair with one hand and passed an imaginary knife over his throat with the other.

'Perfect,' Kazik said. The two of them leaned out the window.

'Death is too good for you, German pig!'

The train passed over a bridge and crossed a road with a warning gate up. A farmer waited on his bicycle for the train to pass.

'Ger-man pig!'

The train stopped. Dozens of men, some of them still in the striped clothes of the concentration camps, jumped from the cars and began to chase a plump peasant girl. She managed to escape. They started to smash the windows and doors of the house next-door. Someone brought a can of kerosene. Two men dragged an old German along the ground. The porch went up in flames. The train whistled and gave a lurch. The men dropped everything and ran to catch it. The train gathered speed and continued westward.

They stopped once more at the Dutch border. Yurik stepped down from the train, picked up a smooth pebble, and put it away for a remembrance. A German stone. He returned to his compartment and began writing a poem :

Today I leave you forever, o cursed land,
....blood,
....hand,
....mud.

Here and now.....................................
I, a parentless boy...............................
..................................of my paternity.
Cursed be you, cruel land, to all eternity.

That was the last line. He finished writing and hid his notebook in his bag. He propped his chin against the window and stared out at the ploughed fields that stretched away from the railway embankment.

A marching band greeted them on the other side of the border with a huge sign that said : WELCOME HOME !

It turned out that a train full of returning Dutch prisoners of war had been expected.

Women in white gave out milk to the children.

19

In Belgium they were put in a camp near the small town of Vise. Yurik and Kazik asked if they could go into town.

'Yes, you may,' Stella said.

The town nestled in hills and its streets went up and down. A woman was mopping the pavement in front of her shop. It was a summer morning. Yurik hitched up the new canvas trousers that Stella had made for him. 'Look, they wash the pavements here,' he said.

Kazik walked by his side, shuffling along in a pair of Viktor's old loafers. They stopped by a café on a street corner to look at an ancient bicycle with a big front wheel, on which the seat was mounted, and a small rear one.

'It's attached to the pavement,' said Yurik, disappointed.

'Don't touch it, they'll yell at us. It must be their sign.'

The boys approached the window of the café. Two women and a small boy were sitting at a table inside. The younger of the two women was feeding the boy. The older one sat looking on with enjoyment.

'They're eating ice cream,' whispered Kazik, his face pressed against the glass.

The boy inside said something to his mother. He threw his spoon on the ground.

His mother said something back to him and wiped his mouth with a handkerchief. His grandmother put on her lace gloves.

'They're looking at us,' whispered Kazik.

'Just look at those gloves. They must be rich.'

'Perhaps they'll give us some ice cream?'

'They won't,' said Yurik, 'let's go.' He pulled at his brother. 'Come on.'

'Uncle Viktor gave me ten francs,' Kazik said, fingering them in his pocket. 'Don't walk so fast, I can't keep up with you.'

'Then take off your shoes and carry them,' Yurik said.

They stopped by the window of a toy shop.

'How much is ten francs, a lot?'

'I'd like a car like that,' said Yurik half under his breath, as though the toys would disappear from the window if he spoke too loud. 'Should we go in?'

'Maybe it costs ten francs.'

'Let's go in.'

They opened the door and stood there. Kazik put his shoes on the floor and slipped into them. '*Monsieur?*' said the salesman, singing the last syllable. He looked down at them and smiled. '*Que voulez-vous, enfants?*'

'He's asking us what we want,' Yurik guessed.

Kazik stepped up to the glass counter and laid two five-franc coins on it. He pointed at the red car in the window. The salesman took it out and ran it back and forth on the counter. He flashed his ten fingers at them once, twice, and a third time.

'Thirty,' whispered Yurik. Kazik went to the counter and quietly took back his two coins. There were tears in his eyes. Yurik pulled him by the hand. 'Let's go.'

'Wait a minute, *messieurs*,' said the salesman. 'The war is over. Take this as my gift to you and enjoy it. You're

from the refugee camp, I can tell. Here, take it, it's yours.'
He spoke in French. The boys didn't understand a word.

He took the car and handed it to Kazik. Kazik took it and put his money back on the counter.

'*Non, non,* boys,' said the salesman, giving it back.

At last they understood. They jostled each other towards the door.

'He gave it to us,' Kazik said.

A convoy of tall army trucks passed by the shop. Their drivers were all Negroes.

'Look, Yurik, he's steering with his feet!'

The Negro driver waved hello to them, smiling with his white teeth. They waved back.

Cities, towns, each with its own soup kitchen.

Namiers was the name of a town. It was near Tiras. The orphans from Belgium and France had already been sent to Palestine. In the special camp were children still waiting for their parents.

Yurik and Kazik were already undressed. 'Are they coming tomorrow?'

'That's what the director said.'

Pani Replawicz's son Rishek was still taking off his trousers. He finally got them off and turned to the wall. It was a cloudless night. Kazik yawned. Yurik got out of bed and went over to him.

'Should we scare him tonight?' he asked in a whisper.

'Maybe just a little.'

'What will you do?'

'I'll make scary sounds.'

'All right,' Yurik said.

'Rishek,' whispered Yurik. The boy turned to look at him. 'I know it's you,' said Rishek after a moment's silence.

'I can see you,' he said, trying to smile. 'I can see you standing there. Yurik? Yurik? I know it's you walking. Yurik? Yurik, answer me!' Just then the ghost lifted its arms and spread them out wide.

'Aaaahh!' Rishek cried out in terror. 'I know it's you! I tell you I know! Stop!'

'Death,' whispered Kazik eerily from his bed. 'Death, death, death, death, death . . .'

Walpurgis Night had begun.

The parents were brought by car the next day.

'More suitcases and bundles,' grumbled Yurik.

'Are you starting up already?' Stella asked. 'If you don't like it, don't get dressed.'

Yurik hated all the packages, crates and valises. Now that the camp was full of adults there were constant trips to Brussels where the days were spent running back and forth between offices. Viktor demanded money for the boys. Stella demanded clothing. There were shouts and arguments.

Yurik hated these trips.

'You don't have to come with us and you can feed and support yourself too,' Stella said angrily, hiking up her dress and sitting down on the steps of the building.

'Aunt Stella,' he tried to dissuade her. 'On the street?'

'Don't you worry,' she reassured him. 'Your aunt knows how to be a lady when she wants to, and she knows how to sit on steps too. You can go and get me a chair if you feel like it. Can you see if Viktor is coming? All we need now is for it to rain.'

There were problems about getting to Palestine. Stella couldn't get an immigration certificate from the Jewish Agency.

'But it's me who saved them! For six years of the war!' she shouted in Polish, Yiddish, German and Russian.

'She's a mother to them.' Viktor banged on the table. There were more hallways, and steps, and offices, and officials behind desks who were terribly sorry but . . . and more slamming of doors.

Wherever there was a Joint, a Jewish Agency office, or a soup kitchen, there was a bathroom. Kazik always knew where to find it and would lead his brother there.

Stella wasn't given a visa to Palestine. They promised to try to fit her into one of the next groups.

'You could go illegally,' suggested Viktor. 'There are ships all the time.'

'No,' she declined. 'I didn't get through the whole war just to have the English blow me up on some stupid ocean near Palestine. Anything but that.'

'Then let them go by themselves. And stop crying. In a minute, they'll start too. I swear to God, this is a madhouse.'

Stella packed their bags and went on weeping. Viktor handed her a handkerchief. 'That's enough.' She took it and wiped her nose.

'Yurik,' she said, 'listen to me carefully. Tomorrow you're not going to have an aunt any more to explain everything to you. In this bag I'm putting the food for the rest of your trip. All the clothes are in Kazik's bag. I'm keeping your good clothes with me, because if they see them in Palestine they won't give you any of their own. If they don't anyway, write to me and I'll send you these. Otherwise I'll sell them. Do you have all the addresses I wrote down for you? Your uncle's in London too? Pani Replawicz will give you money for a telegram. She promised to look after you on the way. If we can find that uncle in London things will start looking up. He was very rich before the war. I'm putting the sandwiches for the first day of your trip right here; make sure you don't sit on them. Where did you put your notebook? Whatever you do, don't lose it. Yurik, you have to be an adult now, do you understand? You're leaving in the morning. Don't worry, Kazhiula. I'll be coming soon myself, and then we'll be together again. Do you promise? And wear your woollen sweaters, they say it's cold at night in Palestine even in the summer. Do you hear me, Yurik? Don't try to be a big hero there. You know that your health was never good as a child.'

'Sell the cigarettes in France,' Viktor put in, 'and you'll have enough money for stamps and travelling expenses. And don't forget to send us a postcard when you get there, or else your aunt will worry.'

'Right, right,' Yurik said.

'And don't you dare tell your true ages,' Stella reminded them. 'You were born in 'thirty-five and you in 'thirty-three. Remember, or else they'll send you off to work and you won't have any time for school. You're not like other children, you know. You lost six years in the war.'

Kazik cuddled up to her wordlessly.

20

Kazik refused to go to Palestine. Twenty or more trucks filled with adults and children waited for him impatiently.

Kazik sobbed bitterly. 'I won't go without you. I won't!'

Stella tried to calm him. 'Kazhiula, I'll come to join you in a few months.' There were tears in her eyes. 'I'll come, Kazhiula. Don't cry. Go now. You're holding everyone up.'

A crowd of people and officials gathered around them. A

woman blew her nose with emotion. Yurik was already in the truck. A tall official went over to Kazik and reached out his hand. 'Come, son, I'm talking to you as one man to another. You have my word of honour that the next certificate to Palestine that we get here in Brussels will be your aunt's. Let's shake on it.'

He helped Stella put Kazik on the truck. 'Be a brave boy now. We need your kind in Palestine.'

The trucks started their motors. Stella said goodbye. 'Be well, Kazhiula, be well, Yurik. Don't order him around. Take good care of him. Listen to what Yurik tells you, Kazhiula. He's your big brother now.' The convoy began to move. 'Yurik,' Stella remembered, 'see a dentist about your tooth the first thing. Otherwise they'll have to pull it out. Don't forget!' She slipped her arm through Viktor's and the two of them stood there waving handkerchiefs.

Yurik puked the first time on the way to Paris. No one noticed. He threw up between the side of the truck and its canvas top.

'Yurik.'

'What do you want?'

Kazik was squirming in his seat. 'It's not my problem,' Yurik said angrily. 'You should have gone in Brussels before we left.'

'Yurik, I can't . . .'

'Ask one of the counsellors.'

'You ask.'

'I can't, I'm too nauseous.'

They reached Paris towards evening. On the walls of the working-class suburbs someone had scrawled : JEWS TO THE GAS CHAMBERS ! In French. And German. And Polish.

'Yurik, come quick, the Eiffel Tower !'

Yurik skipped to the other side of the truck and managed to catch a glimpse of it.

There were three lifts in the hotel. They went up and down and up. They were given room 733 on the seventh floor.

'Seven plus three plus three again makes thirteen,' said Yurik. 'We'll have good luck.' He turned the key and opened the door.

'Look, two beds! And look at that mirror on the wardrobe.'

'And a carpet,' Kazik marvelled. 'Look, here's another door.'

'Does it open?'

'A bathtub!'

'See if there's hot water.'

Kazik turned both taps. 'There is. We'll be like kings!'

'Where's the small bag?' Yurik asked. He peered into it. 'Did you sit on it?'

'Not me,' Kazik said.

'Here, throw this out.'

'Where should I throw it?'

'In a dustbin.'

'Aunt Stella said not to order me around,' Kazik complained.

'All right, I'll go and look for one,' said Yurik. 'But make the beds while I'm gone.'

He went downstairs but couldn't find a dustbin. There was a restaurant on the ground floor. People sat eating at little tables while waiters hurried back and forth. There were lights all around.

Yurik slipped outside. He looked up and down both pavements before dumping the contents of the bag into the street. The squashed sandwiches fell out first; then came some hardboiled eggs mixed with shells and some tomato juice. He turned the bag on its side and scraped it out.

In the morning, he thought, they would yell again about

how the Jews were always spreading filth. Let them yell. There wasn't a dustbin to put it in. Anyway, they were leaving tomorrow. Nobody would know it was him.

'Have you ridden in a lift yet?'

'I've already ridden in two,' Kazik said.

Yurik turned on the hot water tap and took off his clothes. He stood opposite the mirror and beat his smooth chest with his fists. 'Look how handsome I am,' he boasted. 'Or am I?'

They got off the train to change lines. It was two o'clock in the morning. The huge station rumbled with the wheels of arriving and departing trains. Announcements came over the loudspeaker. People walked hurriedly from platform to platform or dozed on the benches in the waiting-rooms. Blinking lights kept changing colour. Miniature locomotives pulled trolleys loaded with suitcases.

Lyons, Yurik read on a large sign.

There were French soldiers, English soldiers, American soldiers. Yurik and Kazik strolled back and forth with their bags. For a while they followed some German prisoners of war who were walking with their hands up while a Negro soldier prodded them with his rifle butt. Suddenly the two boys halted.

'Look,' said Kazik, putting down his bag, 'those soldiers have fezes on their heads.'

'And swords.'

'Perhaps they're mounted camel troops from the Sahara?'

'They must take their camels on the baggage cars, like horses,' guessed Yurik.

'Look, one of them's talking,' Kazik whispered.

'He just sat down,' Yurik said.

'Hurry!' said a man, grabbing hold of them. 'What are you doing here?' He got them back on the train just as it was beginning to move.

'Who's in charge of you?'

'We're in charge of ourselves,' Yurik said.

The man's wife spread some blankets for them on a bench and put them to sleep.

Marseilles, Yurik read. In the station they met Pan G.

He was happy to see them. 'Hello there, boys,' he said, reaching out to shake hands.

They didn't answer.

'Aren't you going to say hello to me either?' he asked Kazik.

'Let's go,' Yurik said. They went to the trucks. The trucks brought them to a camp outside the town.

They sailed in a ship from Toulon. Everyone stood on deck and sang the *Hatikvah*.

'Is that the same song they always sing?'

'Yes,' said Yurik. 'It's their anthem.'

A French officer stood at attention on the pier below and saluted.

Yurik was seasick. Kazik befriended some sailors from the engine room. The ship docked in Haifa. The sea was blue. White houses climbed up the ridges of Mount Carmel from the bay. The children were brought by the British police to some cabins for the medical inspection.

'Have you been circumcised?' a boy asked them. 'Whoever hasn't been circumcised gets it done now.'

'Our grandparents did it for us,' Yurik said.

'I was circumcised too,' the boy said worriedly, 'but then they changed me back again when I was on the Polish side.'

After the medical inspection they were ushered into a large room full of tables behind which sat the representatives of the various Jewish political parties. The children stood in line.

'What's going on in there?' Kazik asked.

Yurik shrugged.

'Look at that Jew,' whispered Kazik, pointing to a man with a long beard and a hat.

'Don't point,' said Yurik, pulling down his arm. 'It's not nice.'

'What party do you belong to?' a man asked them. Yurik didn't understand the question.

'You have to choose a youth movement for yourselves,' he explained.

'What movements are there?'

The man counted them off and ended with Gordonia, named after the Zionist leader Aharon David Gordon.

Yurik nudged his brother with an elbow. 'Did you hear that?' he whispered. 'There's one for General Gordon.'

Kazik nodded.

'If it isn't any trouble,' he told the man behind the table, 'we'll take Gordon's party.'

Thanks to the recommendations of some people who knew the two boys from Bergen-Belsen, Yurik and Kazik were separated from the group of children assigned to an agricultural work camp and were sent off to school at Kibbutz Gannim.

21

'I'm telling you again, Yosef, I think the older boy should be put in the eighth grade and the younger one in the sixth. There's no doubt they'll catch up. The younger one can certainly do it, and if his brother is as capable as they say, so can he. They'll never fit into one of the lower grades socially, and that's terribly important. Even the children in the eighth grade will all be a year younger than the older boy.'

'What are you talking about, he was born . . . wait a minute, I have it written down somewhere. He was born in 'thirty-three.'

'Oh, I forgot to tell you,' the house mother recalled. 'They secretly told me that each of them is really two years older than his official age. Because of the war over there they had to falsify their ages.'

'I see they were in some children's home in Belgium,' said the teacher, looking through the papers.

'Apparently they learned a few things there. The children who came to us from Russia via Tehran were savages by comparison.'

'Wait a minute,' he interrupted her. 'Why don't you bring them in now? We'll test them and assign them to a class right now.'

The house mother went out and came back with Yurik and Kazik. They bowed when they entered the room. 'Good morning, sir,' they said.

'Have a seat,' he said to them in Polish. 'How are you? We don't bow here on the kibbutz, and we don't bother to say "sir". You'll get used to it.'

Yurik was afraid of tests.

'Have you studied any history?'

'Yes, in Bergen-Belsen. And in the ghetto too.'

'What did you learn about?'

'About Greece and Rome. And also about the Franks,' he recalled.

'Did you study history in school too?'

'No, we never got as far as that.'

'I see,' said the teacher. 'And arithmetic?'

'Fractions.'

'Decimals too?'

Yurik hesitated. He wasn't sure if the teacher meant points and chose not to answer.

'Can you tell me how much one-half plus one-third is?'

He was afraid of tests. He tried to think of fractions, of equal signs. What did you multiply by what? Oh yes, he remembered, you had to find the common denominator. Multiply the bottoms by the bottoms. He mumbled something.

'All right, that'll do,' said the teacher. 'You can go now. I'll think it over,' he told the house mother.

'Have you ever seen two such boys?' she said enthusiastically when they were gone. 'And the way they bowed, not like our own little wild Indians. Do you know what's bowled them over the most so far? That each gets two eggs in every omelette and his own toothbrush.'

'Well, well, they'll get used to that too,' said the teacher, getting up to go.

She rose to follow him, smoothing out her apron. 'You know,' she continued, 'they even asked me where the shops were here. I explained to them that there are no shops on a kibbutz and that we all live and work together here, and learn together, and eat together in one dining-room. Then I told them that we were farmers and shepherds here. In their world, you know, a shepherd is the epitome of backwardness.'

'Are you coming to eat?' asked the teacher.

'Yes,' she said, 'let's go together.' She shut the door behind her. 'The older boy asked me what happens if you steal. They must have learned a few things about the seamy side of life in that war. They've been through so much, so terribly much.'

GREETINGS AND WELCOME TO YOUR HOMELAND,

THE KIBBUTZ.

'What does it say here?' asked Yurik, looking at the inside cover of the book.

'It's a dedication,' explained the house mother. 'It says that the kibbutz is presenting you with this Bible on the occasion of your arrival in your homeland.'

'Is this the same book as our Polish Bible?' asked Yurik.

'There are two testaments,' she explained, 'the Old and the New. The Christians generally believe more in the New Testament. But actually, the whole world recognizes the Old Testament, which is ours. Besides we Jews, the British like to read it especially.'

'Why don't they let Jews come to Palestine?'

'Let's leave that for tomorrow,' she said. 'It's already late. Goodnight, boys.'

'Goodnight.'

There were two other beds in their room, but these were empty. The children who slept in them were also not from kibbutz families, and had gone home for the school holidays. Yurik looked out of the screened window. All day long he'd had the feeling that this window was a large painted landscape with its thin trees, its red tile roofs, and its woods all broken up into little squares like sections on a sample that someone had coloured in. The moon was shining so brightly outside that he could read by its light.

'No, you can't.'

'Come here and I'll show you.'

Kazik put his hand out to the light. 'Maybe you could,' he conceded, 'but if it was a newspaper, only the headlines.'

'I bet you I could read the whole newspaper.'

They argued a while, shook hands on the bet, and went back to their beds.

Yurik lay dreaming. He knew why he hadn't been killed in the war and why everything had happened the way it had. It was because he was the son of the great emperor of China who ruled beyond the Great Wall.

His bed was on a stage, surrounded by paper dragons and strange deities. The Chinamen were his father the emperor's Mandarins. They were all great sages and wise men. Each had a wispy white Chinese beard and a mandarin orange on his hat, which was why they were called Mandarins. They had put him to sleep on orders from his father so that he might dream about the war. When he awoke again he too would be a great wise man and would know how to rule the yellow millions whose emperor he would be upon his father's death. And he too would have his own son put to sleep behind a white curtain like himself.

Everybody, even Kazik, had been created expressly for his dream. In reality they didn't exist. He was destined for greatness and would be a great emperor one day. He could feel it, for instance, when he looked up at the stars at night. It was no wonder that he had survived. He would always escape every danger. When the dream was over, he'd go home. His people were waiting for him. A magnificent ceremony would be held in the imperial court, a great Chinese pageant in his honour.

He fell asleep. Hands in his trouser pockets, he strolled through the streets of Warsaw. He had forgotten how he had once loved this city with its horse-drawn carriages.

In Palestine there weren't even any trolley-buses.

He ambled along with his hands in his pockets. A red trolley-bus passed him ringing its bell. Bright neon lights kept changing colour. The lights of a ship floated down the Vistula.

The emperor of China was homesick.

The emperor of China had never read the Bible.

The emperor of China loved – gratuitously, for its own sake – whatever the Mandarins controlling his dream taught him to love.

The emperor of China would have to conceal what he had loved, for now the wise Mandarins would teach him to love his new land.

22

Kazik strode down the cypress-lined lane carrying a large cardboard box under one arm. Yurik walked beside him.

'What's my name again?' the younger brother asked.

Yurik stopped to think. 'I can't remember,' he said.

Kazik spied the house mother going up the steps of a nearby bungalow and called to her. 'Pani Rita, what's my name?'

She smiled at him. 'Your name's Yoram. Yo-ram. It's time you remembered. And you can call me just plain Rita. What's your name?' she asked Yurik.

'That's easy,' said Jerzy Henryk. 'My name's Arnon.'

She entered the bungalow and they kept on walking down the path.

'Yo-ram, Yo-ram,' Kazik said over and over.

'Should we show them all our things?' asked Yurik.

'Let's show them,' said Kazik. They climbed the three steps to the room.

The three boys who were there watched them come in silently.

'They're from those who were left after the Germans killed six million,' said one of the boys in Hebrew. 'They're refugees. We're supposed to play with them. My mother told me.'

'Have you talked to them?'

'Yes, in English.'

'They can talk it?'

'The big one knows a little. The little one just knows Polish.'

Yurik took the cardboard box from Kazik and emptied it out on the floor. There were soldiers, cars, tanks, guns, and troop carriers.

'*This is auto, can trrrr alone,*' he said in English, pointing to one of the vehicles. He pointed to himself and Kazik : '*This is from the Germans, we take.*' He took one of the cars and began to wind it up.

'*Beautiful?*' he asked.

'*Yes.*'

'*I know English from Bergen-Belsen.*'

'Tell him that we learn English at school.'

'You tell him.'

'I don't know how.'

'*We learn English little in the school,*' said the third boy.

A month went by.

'You collect these . . .' Yurik had to say it in English.

'*Stamps?*'

'Yes.'

'Hmmm,' said Yurik.

Gabbi and Yosi began putting the stamps back in their albums. They put the albums away in their lockers.

'We are a kibbutz,' Yurik said. 'On a kibbutz, come on, how do you say. . . .' He went back to English again. *'You see, when I have one horse, you have one horse. When I have two horse, you have two horse. This is kibbutz. Right?'*

'Right.'

'You have many *stamps*,' he said. 'Give me a little. It is not nice that on the kibbutz you have many *stamps* and I have not any.'

'In Hebrew stamps are *bulim*,' Yosi taught him. He conferred with Gabbi in a whisper. They opened their albums and leafed through them. 'We'll give him some from here,' decided Yosi.

Yurik received fifteen stamps and began a new collection.

Yurik was put in the eighth grade and Kazik in the sixth. At first Yurik studied only English and arithmetic, but by the end of the year he had caught up in the other subjects as well, lagging behind only in Hebrew grammar, composition and culture. Kazik refused to apply himself. He would slip out into the yard to look at the cows or to drive the handyman's wagon.

Yurik sat in his room, trying to do an arithmetic problem. The house mother came in. 'There's a telegram for you, Arnon,' she said. Yurik took the envelope from her and opened it.

Your father has arrived from Russia. His letter follows. Anna.

Aunt Anna. Papa had come back. She must have got their address from their relative in London. He read it again.

Your father has arrived from Russia.
Your father has arrived
Your father

A chill ran over his body. The letters on the paper grew blurred.

'Did you see how pale he got, Rita?' Yosi said.

Yurik ran to Kazik's cottage. On the way he threw up his afternoon snack on the lawn.

'Kazik, Papa's alive! We've got a telegram!'

'Let me see,' said Kazik. 'Let me hold it myself.'

'But give it back!'

Kazik stood up for his rights. 'It belongs to me too!'

'I'll let you have it till tomorrow,' said Yurik, 'and after that you'll keep the envelope and I'll keep the telegram, because I'm bigger.'

Their father wrote : *My darling boys, it's a great miracle to have found you both alive. Let us never forget my wife, your mother, who was murdered by the fiends. . . .*
Dear father, wrote Kazik in a round, childish script. *Dear father,* Yurik wrote. *Your letters are wonderful,* their father wrote back. *We thought world socialism would solve the Jewish problem wherever Jews lived, and we've paid dearly for our mistake. I'm studying Hebrew.* Kazik signed his letters : *Your youngest son, Kazik (Yoram).*

'Go to the blackboard, Arnon.'

Yurik walked slowly behind the English teacher's desk.

'I want you to write *Once there was a wizard,*' she said.

Yurik took the chalk and wrote *Once there was a wizard.*

It was a hot, dry, desert day.

'Your letters don't have to take off like an airplane,' the teacher said.

Yurik took the eraser and began to rub out what he had written.

'Don't bother,' she said. 'You can sit down. English and German,' she continued, 'are sister languages. Take the word *school*, for example.' She took the chalk and wrote *school* beneath Yurik's pointed script.

'The same word in German is *Schule*. Or take the English word *garden*. In German it's *Garten*. And so on and so forth.'

Yurik raised his hand.

'Yes, what is it?'

'May I leave the class?'

'Yes, but make sure you get back before the bell,' she replied, already used to his strange behaviour. 'Why are you walking behind me?'

'No special reason,' said Yurik. 'I didn't want to have to pass between you and the class.'

The English teacher was taken aback. 'Arnon, what's the matter with you? Are you suffering from the weather?'

But he was already brushing by the blackboard and erasing the German words with a sweep of his hand. He left the classroom.

Daniel came up to him during recess. 'That was some demonstration you staged.'

'When?'

'Don't play innocent with me. You're blushing.'

'You mean with the blackboard? I just happened to rub against it.'

'What a liar!' snorted the boy. 'It's like that time with

the donkey. You'll confess to both some day. Remember that I said so.'

'There's nothing to confess,' Yurik replied. 'I just happened to have my arm on the donkey.'

'You were hugging it madly. It must be one of those queer foreign customs you brought from abroad.'

'You can kiss my arse.'

Yurik fell in love.

'Are you going in there to do your homework now?'

'Yes,' she said.

They sat at one desk and did trigonometry problems together. A dog was barking in the distance. I passed by the classroom and looked in the window. Yurik had just summoned up the courage to put a trembling arm around her.

Neither said anything. Then she threw back her head and smiled at him.

I left the window. My story is finished and a new story, it would seem, is about to begin.

EPILOGUE

I should like to add a few words about the fate of some of the people mentioned in this book.

Ella was killed during the anti-German uprising of the Polish underground in Warsaw.

Anna managed to slip away from the city and to return to it as a medical officer attached to the Polish division that fought with the Red Army. After the war she took a job at a hospital. Her daughter attends Warsaw University.

Doctor M. M. Kosowolski resettled in the Warsaw suburb of Zoliboz. After marrying a former singer, the daughter of an aristocratic Polish family that had fallen on hard times, he broke off his correspondence with his sons in Israel.

Stella – after an unsuccessful visit to her brother in Warsaw and a furious fight with his new wife – married Viktor Finkel, whose relatives in South Africa helped to get them a visa to that country. They settled in Johannesburg, where they soon grew rich thanks to his business acumen and her devoted assistance. Viktor became the owner of a factory, and the two of them quickly learned to treat their several hundred black employees according to local custom. They are still trying to persuade the two boys to come and live with them in South Africa.

Yurik and Kazik received reparation money from the West German government. They were paid five thousand marks each for injuries incurred by the loss of their freedom and the death of their mother.

Pan G. lives in a port city of Israel, where he holds a high position with a shipping company. After his wife's committal to mental hospital, he remarried and became the father of a boy.

Kibbutz Ginegar
1954